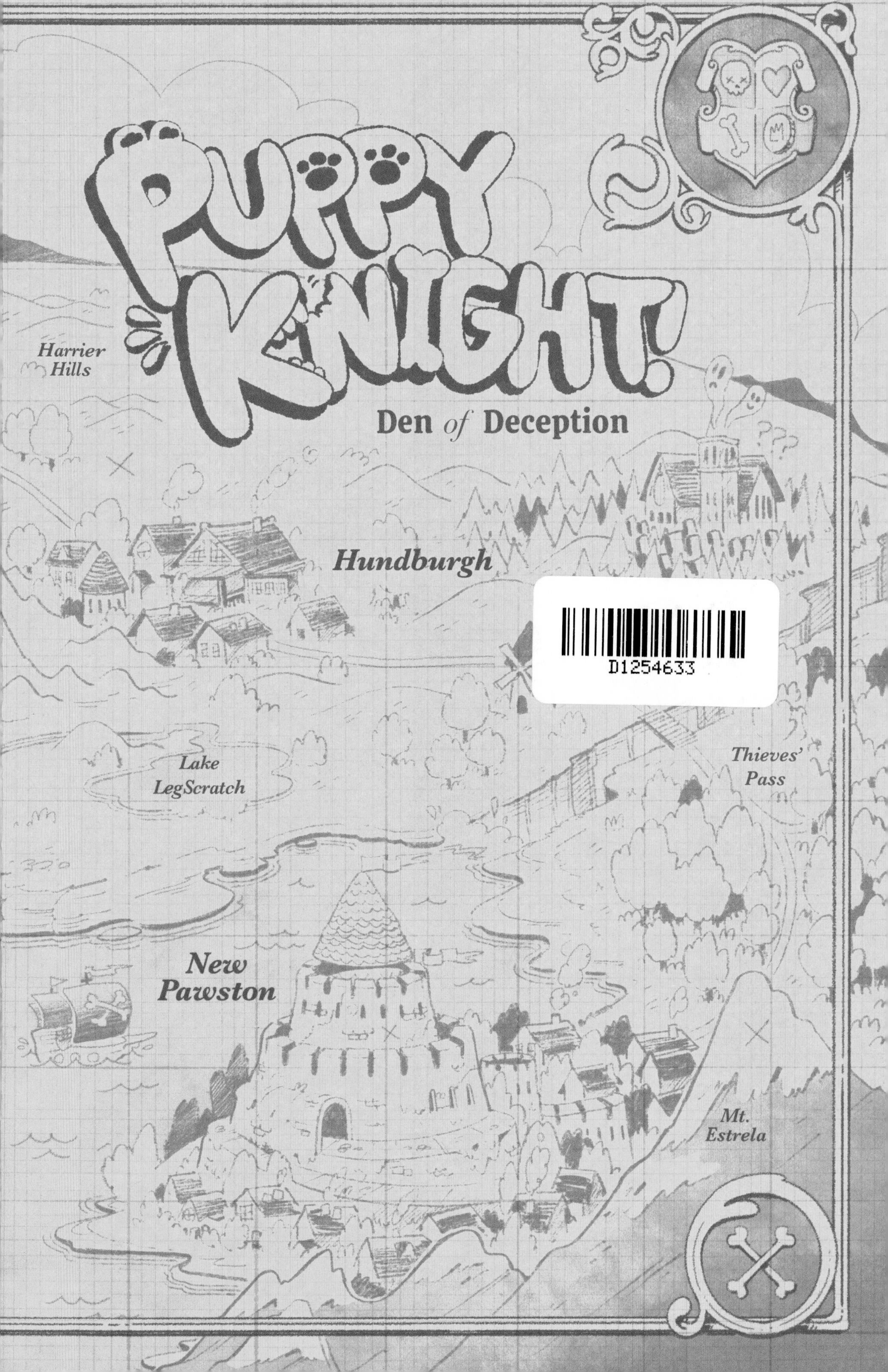
Puppy Knight!
Den of Deception
Harrier Hills
Hundburgh
Lake LegScratch
Thieves' Pass
New Pawston
Mt. Estrela

DEAR READER:

YOU CAN MAKE COMICS
ABOUT ***LITERALLY*** ANYTHING.
GO AND MAKE THEM.

-M. SWEATER + J. CRUZ

SILVER SPROCKET
Avi Ehrlich *Publisher* | Josh PM *General Manager* | Carina Taylor *Production Designer* | Ari Yarwood *Managing Editor* | Simon Jane Crowbrock *Shop Goblin* | Daniel Zhou *Shop Rat* | Raul Higuera-Cortez *Big Head Bandit* | Yasmeen Abedifard *Shop Shroom* | Sarah Maloney *Shop Cat* | Sol Cintron *Fruit Bat*
www.silversprocket.net

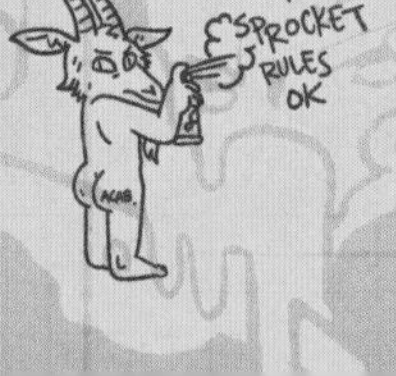
SILVER SPROCKET RULES OK

 ISBN 978-1-945509-83-4.
First Printing, April 2022. Published by Silver Sprocket. 1018 Valencia St, San Francisco, CA 94110, USA.

PUPPY KNIGHT!

Den *of* Deception

Written by MICHAEL SWEATER

Illustrated by JOSUE CRUZ

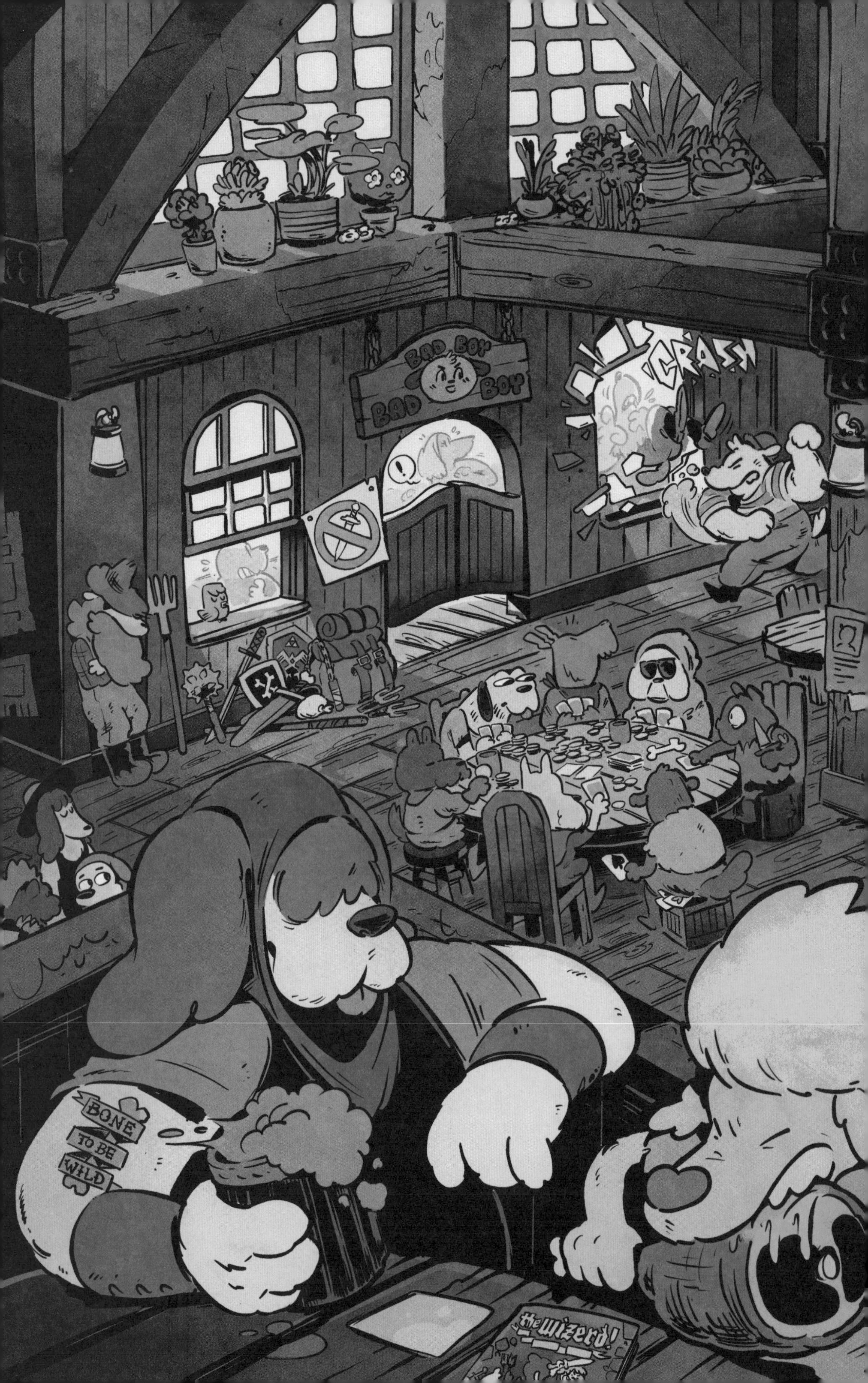
BAD BOY
BAD BOY
CRASH
BONE TO BE WILD
the Wizerd!

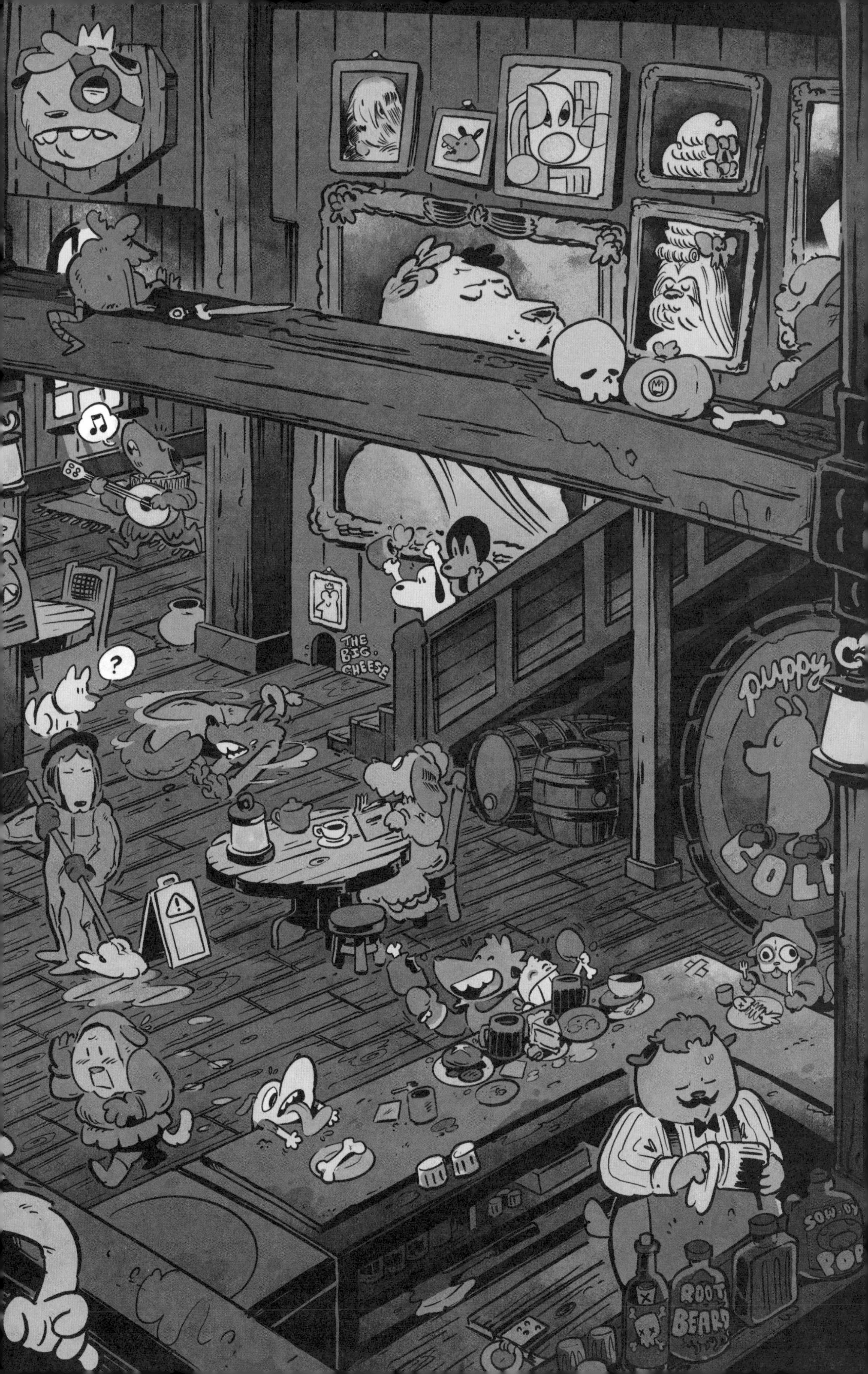

♫
?
THE BIG CHEESE
puppy
ROOT BEARR
SOW-DY POP

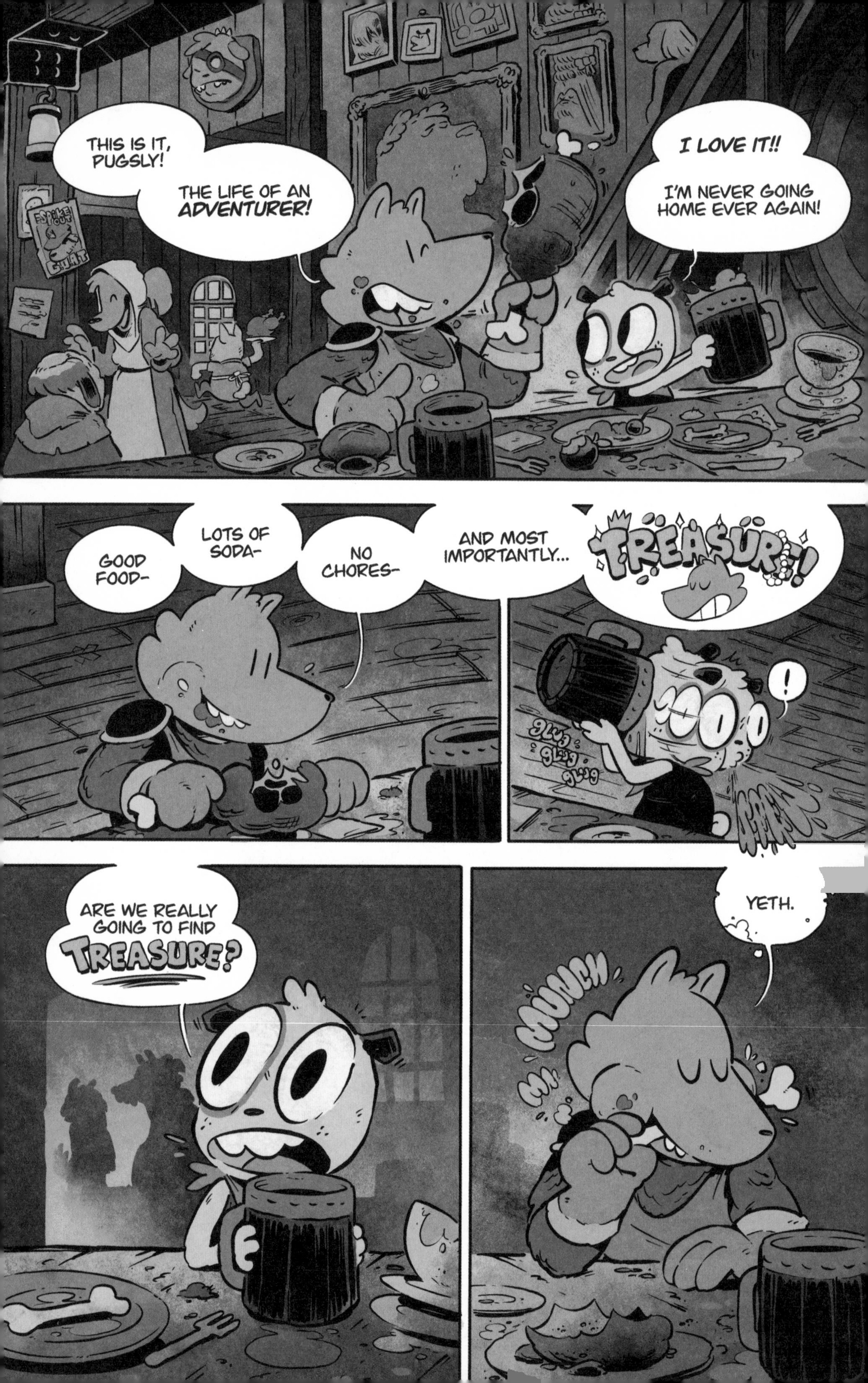
THIS IS IT, PUGSLY!
THE LIFE OF AN ADVENTURER!
I LOVE IT!!
I'M NEVER GOING HOME EVER AGAIN!
GOOD FOOD-
LOTS OF SODA-
NO CHORES-
AND MOST IMPORTANTLY...
TREASURE!
glug glug glug
!
ARE WE REALLY GOING TO FIND TREASURE?
YETH.
MUNCH

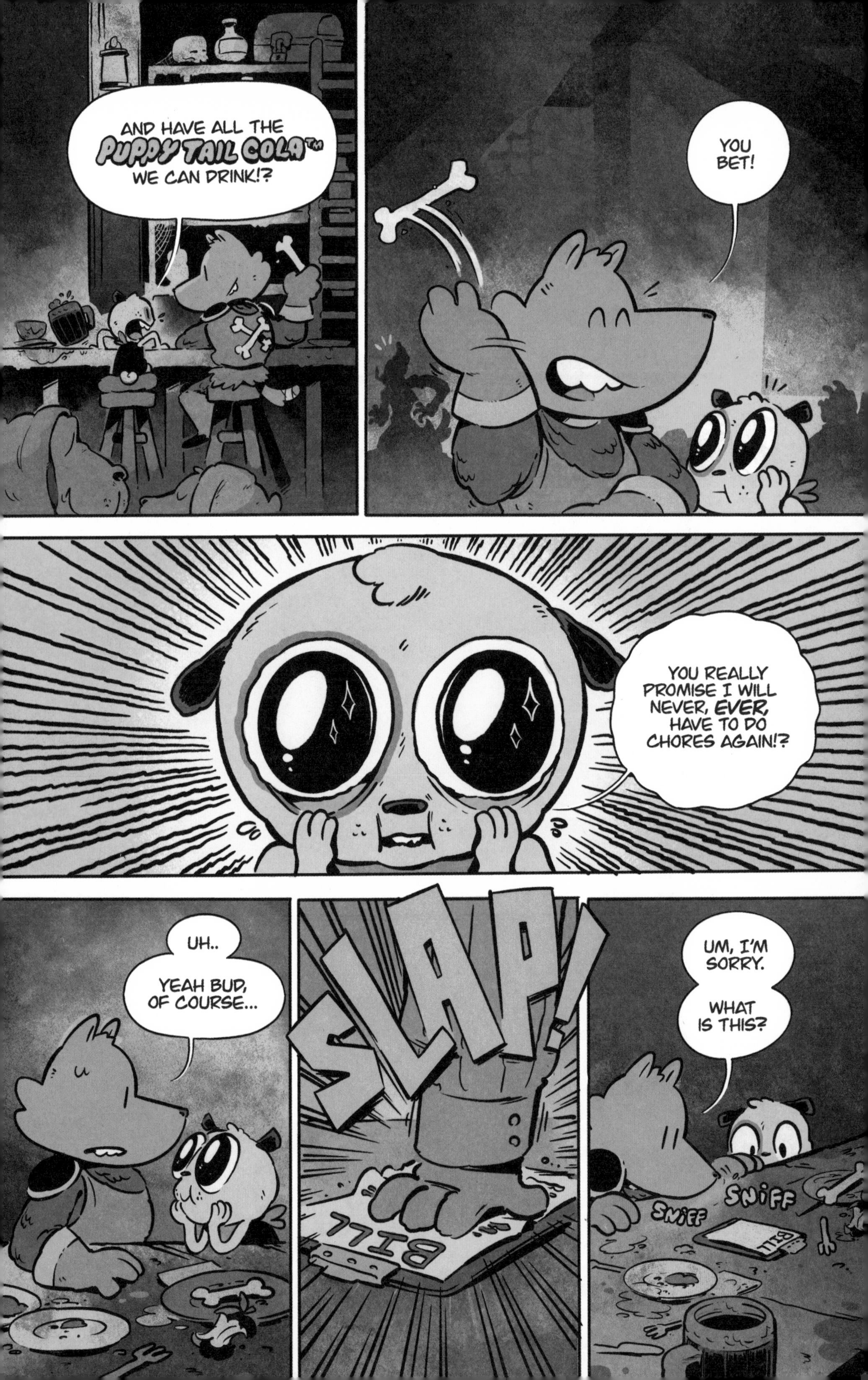
AND HAVE ALL THE PUPPY TAIL COLA™ WE CAN DRINK!?
YOU BET!
YOU REALLY PROMISE I WILL NEVER, EVER, HAVE TO DO CHORES AGAIN!?
UH..
YEAH BUD, OF COURSE...
SLAP!
BILL
UM, I'M SORRY.
WHAT IS THIS?
SNIFF
SNIFF
BILL

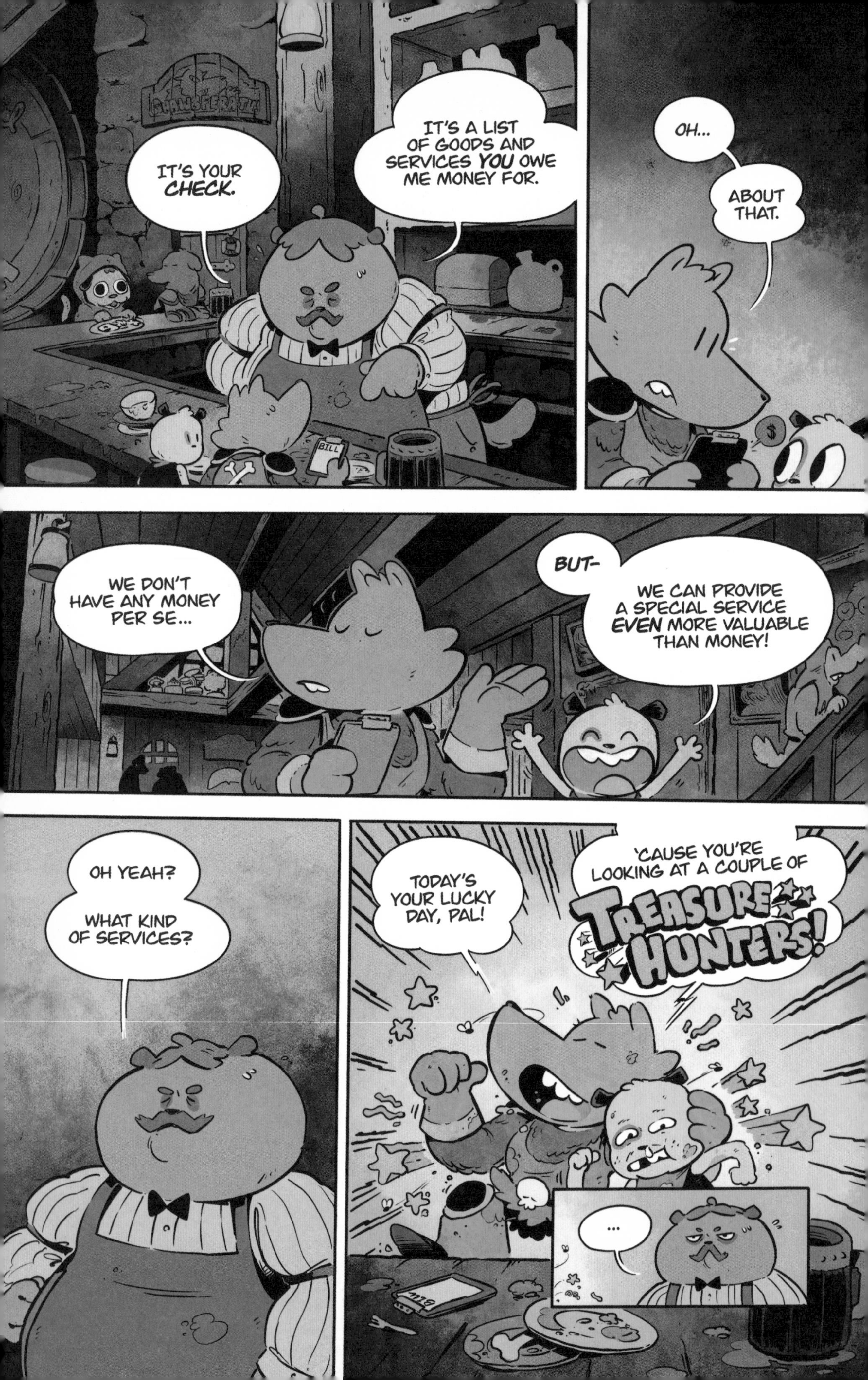

CLAWSFERATU
IT'S YOUR CHECK.
IT'S A LIST OF GOODS AND SERVICES YOU OWE ME MONEY FOR.
BILL
OH...
ABOUT THAT.
WE DON'T HAVE ANY MONEY PER SE...
BUT-
WE CAN PROVIDE A SPECIAL SERVICE EVEN MORE VALUABLE THAN MONEY!
OH YEAH?
WHAT KIND OF SERVICES?
TODAY'S YOUR LUCKY DAY, PAL!
'CAUSE YOU'RE LOOKING AT A COUPLE OF TREASURE HUNTERS!
...
BILL

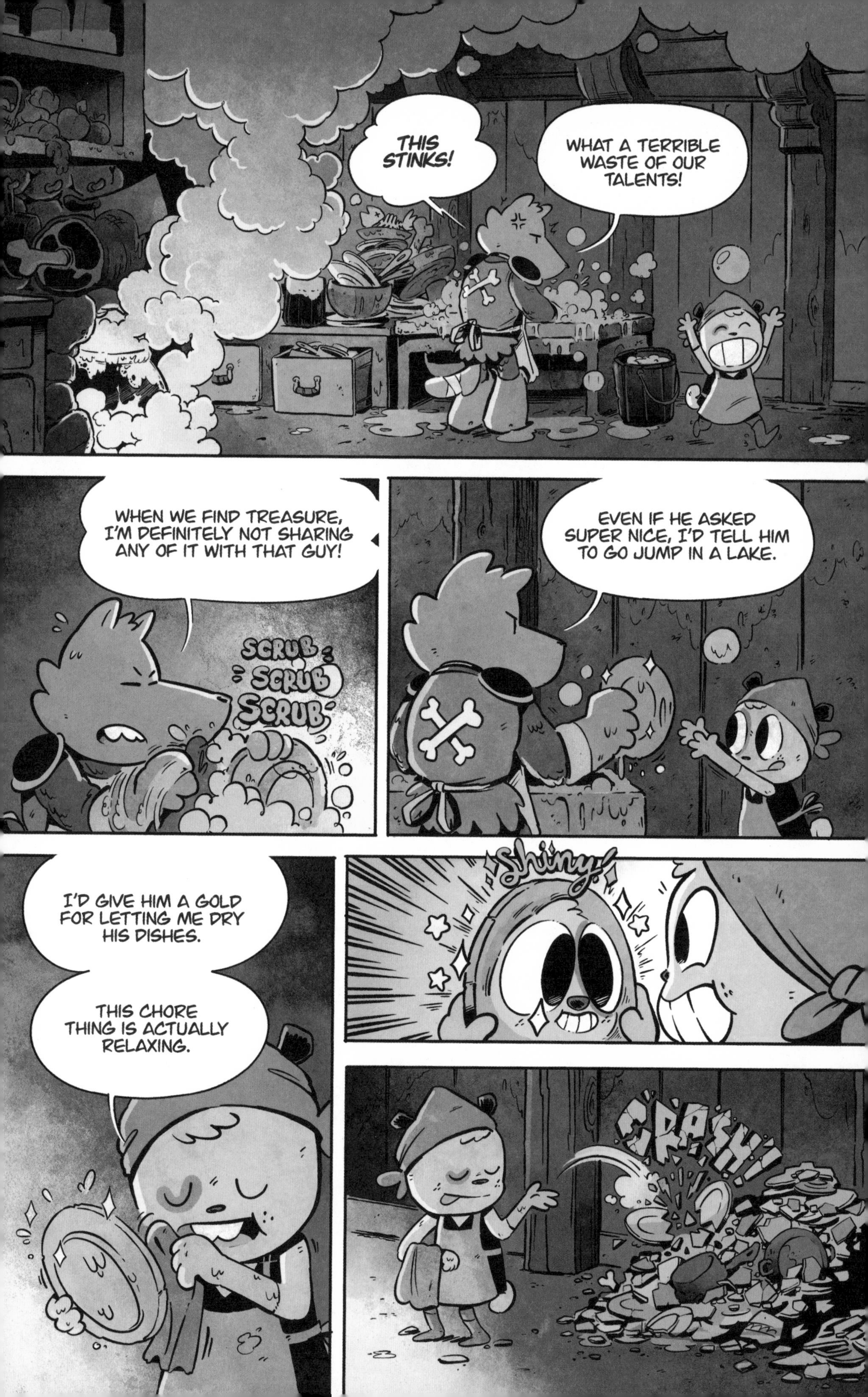
THIS STINKS!
WHAT A TERRIBLE WASTE OF OUR TALENTS!
WHEN WE FIND TREASURE, I'M DEFINITELY NOT SHARING ANY OF IT WITH THAT GUY!
SCRUB SCRUB SCRUB
EVEN IF HE ASKED SUPER NICE, I'D TELL HIM TO GO JUMP IN A LAKE.
I'D GIVE HIM A GOLD FOR LETTING ME DRY HIS DISHES.
THIS CHORE THING IS ACTUALLY RELAXING.
Shiny!
CRASH!

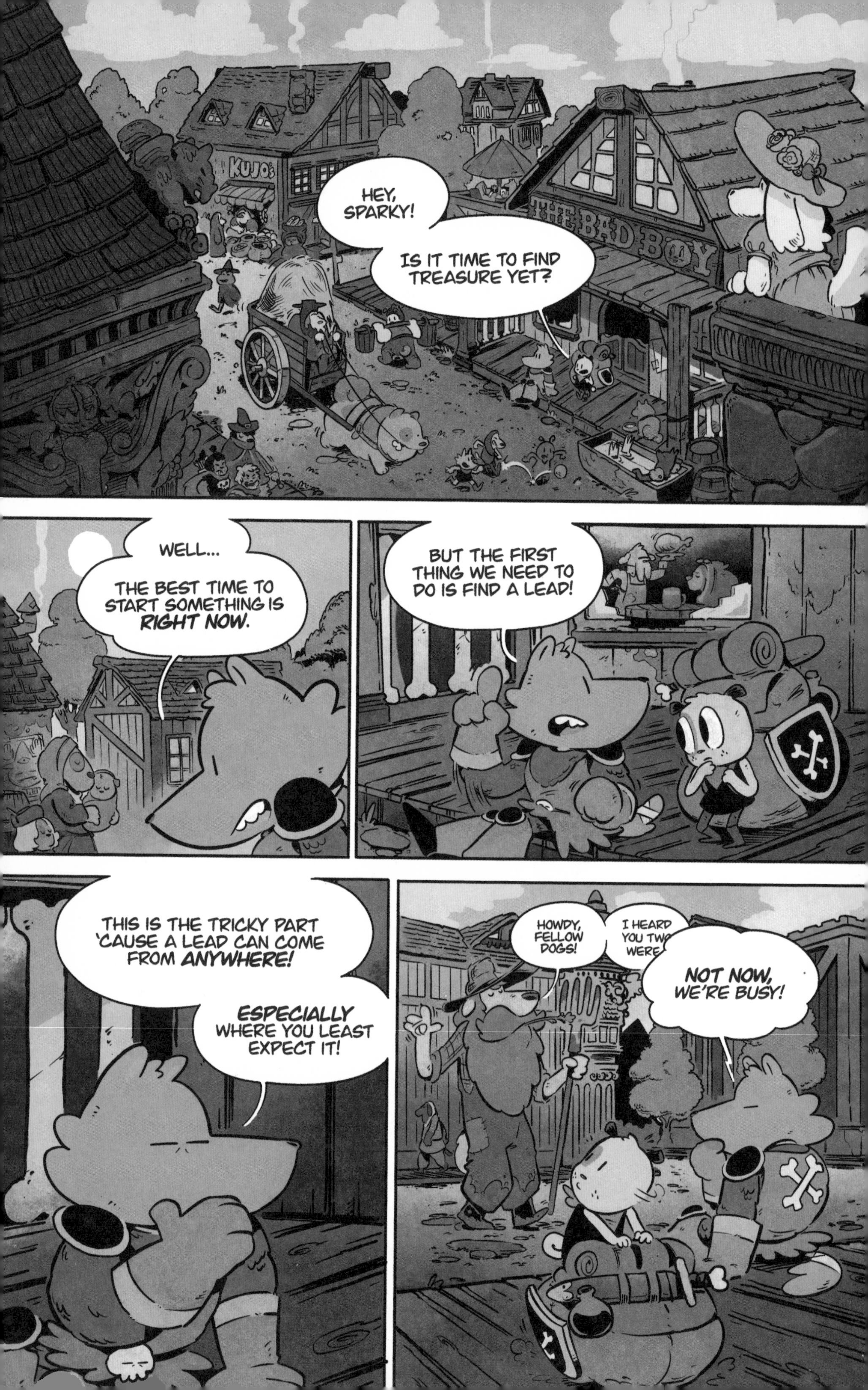
KUJO'S
THE BAD BOY
HEY, SPARKY!
IS IT TIME TO FIND TREASURE YET?
WELL...
THE BEST TIME TO START SOMETHING IS **RIGHT NOW**.
BUT THE FIRST THING WE NEED TO DO IS FIND A LEAD!
THIS IS THE TRICKY PART 'CAUSE A LEAD CAN COME FROM **ANYWHERE!**
ESPECIALLY WHERE YOU LEAST EXPECT IT!
HOWDY, FELLOW DOGS!
I HEARD YOU TWO WERE
NOT NOW, WE'RE BUSY!

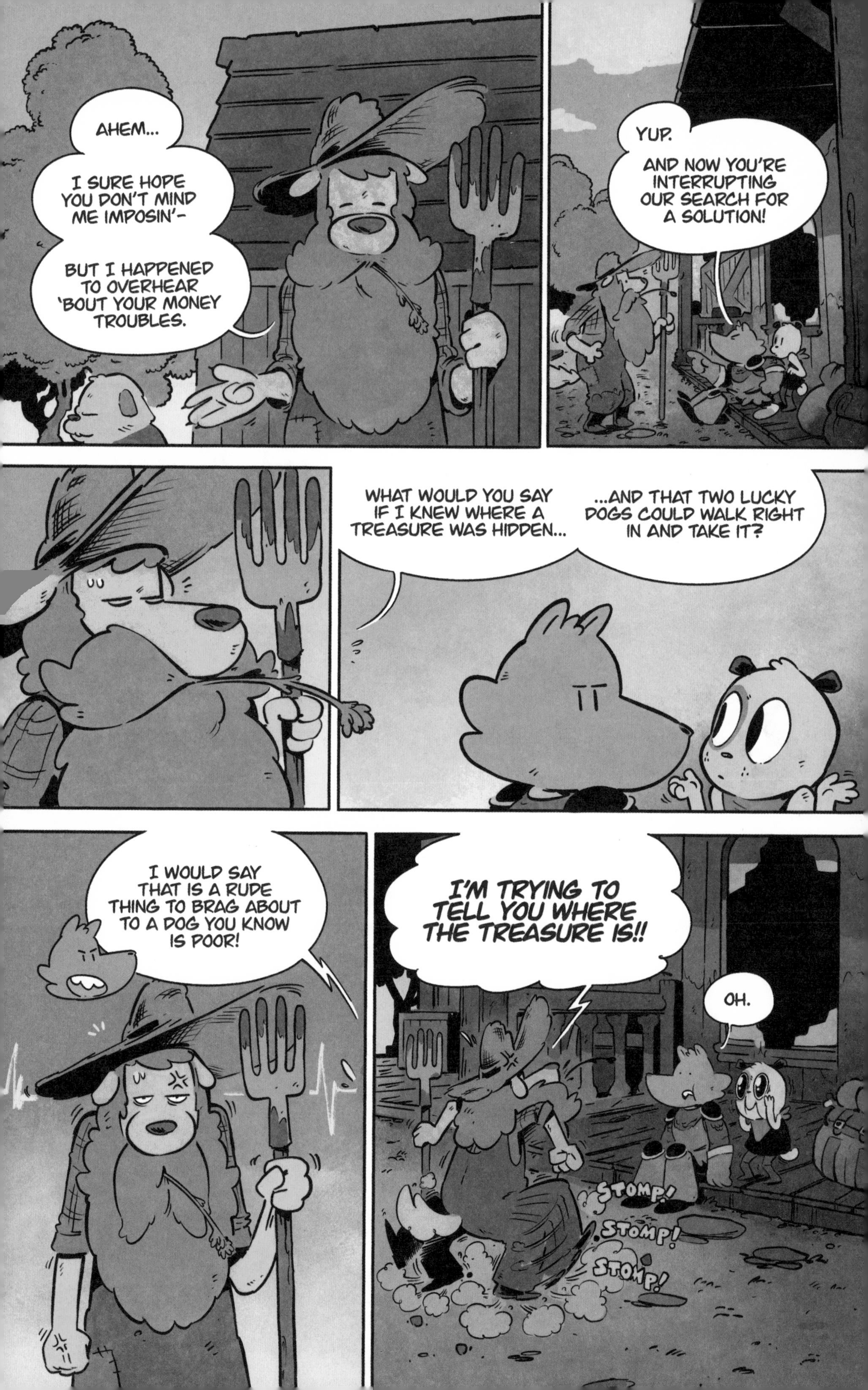
AHEM...
I SURE HOPE YOU DON'T MIND ME IMPOSIN'-
BUT I HAPPENED TO OVERHEAR 'BOUT YOUR MONEY TROUBLES.
YUP.
AND NOW YOU'RE INTERRUPTING OUR SEARCH FOR A SOLUTION!
WHAT WOULD YOU SAY IF I KNEW WHERE A TREASURE WAS HIDDEN...
...AND THAT TWO LUCKY DOGS COULD WALK RIGHT IN AND TAKE IT?
I WOULD SAY THAT IS A RUDE THING TO BRAG ABOUT TO A DOG YOU KNOW IS POOR!
I'M TRYING TO TELL YOU WHERE THE TREASURE IS!!
OH.
STOMP!
STOMP!
STOMP!

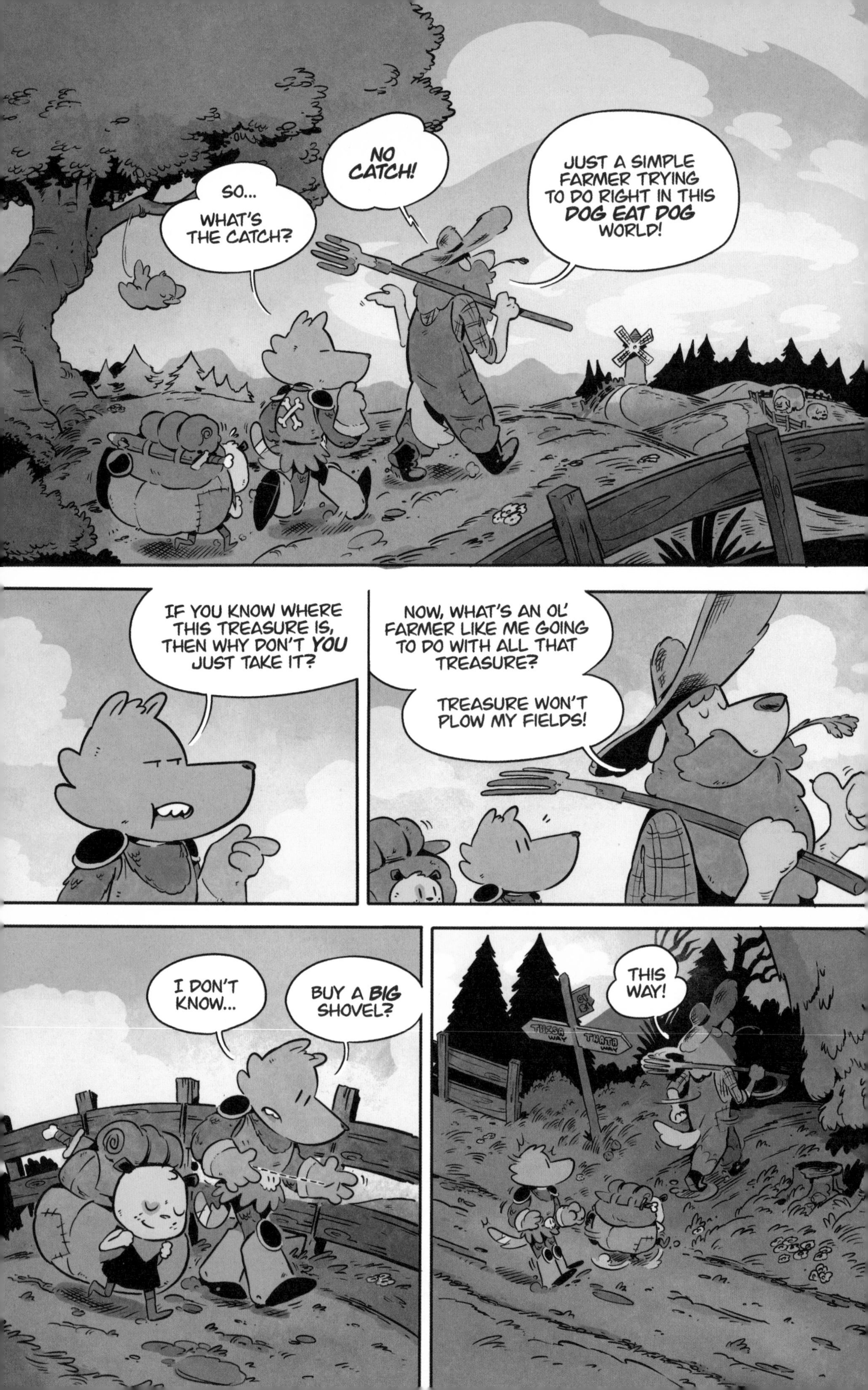
SO...
WHAT'S THE CATCH?
NO CATCH!
JUST A SIMPLE FARMER TRYING TO DO RIGHT IN THIS DOG EAT DOG WORLD!
IF YOU KNOW WHERE THIS TREASURE IS, THEN WHY DON'T YOU JUST TAKE IT?
NOW, WHAT'S AN OL' FARMER LIKE ME GOING TO DO WITH ALL THAT TREASURE?
TREASURE WON'T PLOW MY FIELDS!
I DON'T KNOW...
BUY A BIG SHOVEL?
THIS WAY!
THISA WAY
THATA WAY

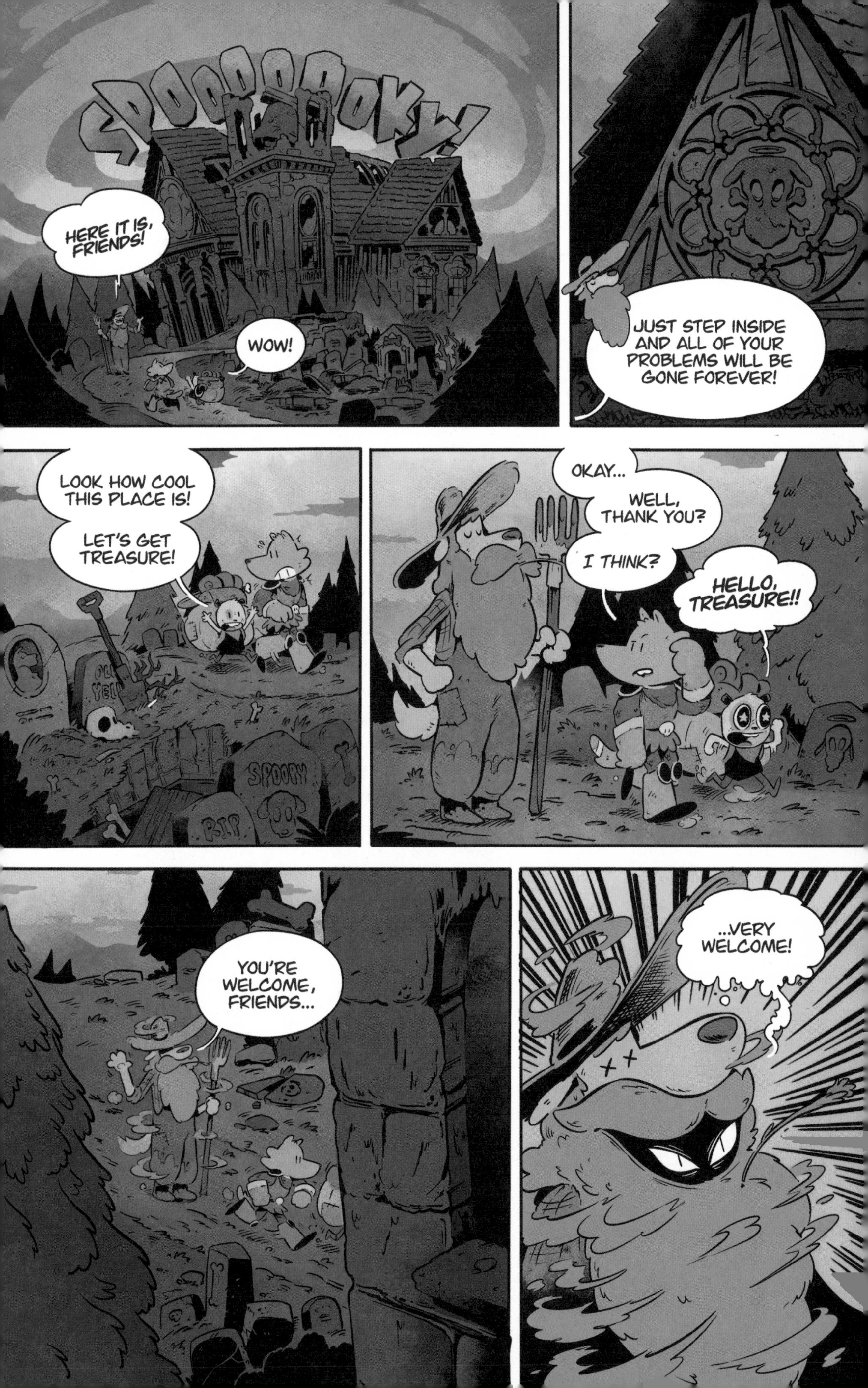
SPOOOOOOKY!
HERE IT IS, FRIENDS!
WOW!
JUST STEP INSIDE AND ALL OF YOUR PROBLEMS WILL BE GONE FOREVER!
LOOK HOW COOL THIS PLACE IS!
LET'S GET TREASURE!
SPOOKY
RIP
OKAY...
WELL, THANK YOU?
I THINK?
HELLO, TREASURE!!
YOU'RE WELCOME, FRIENDS...
...VERY WELCOME!

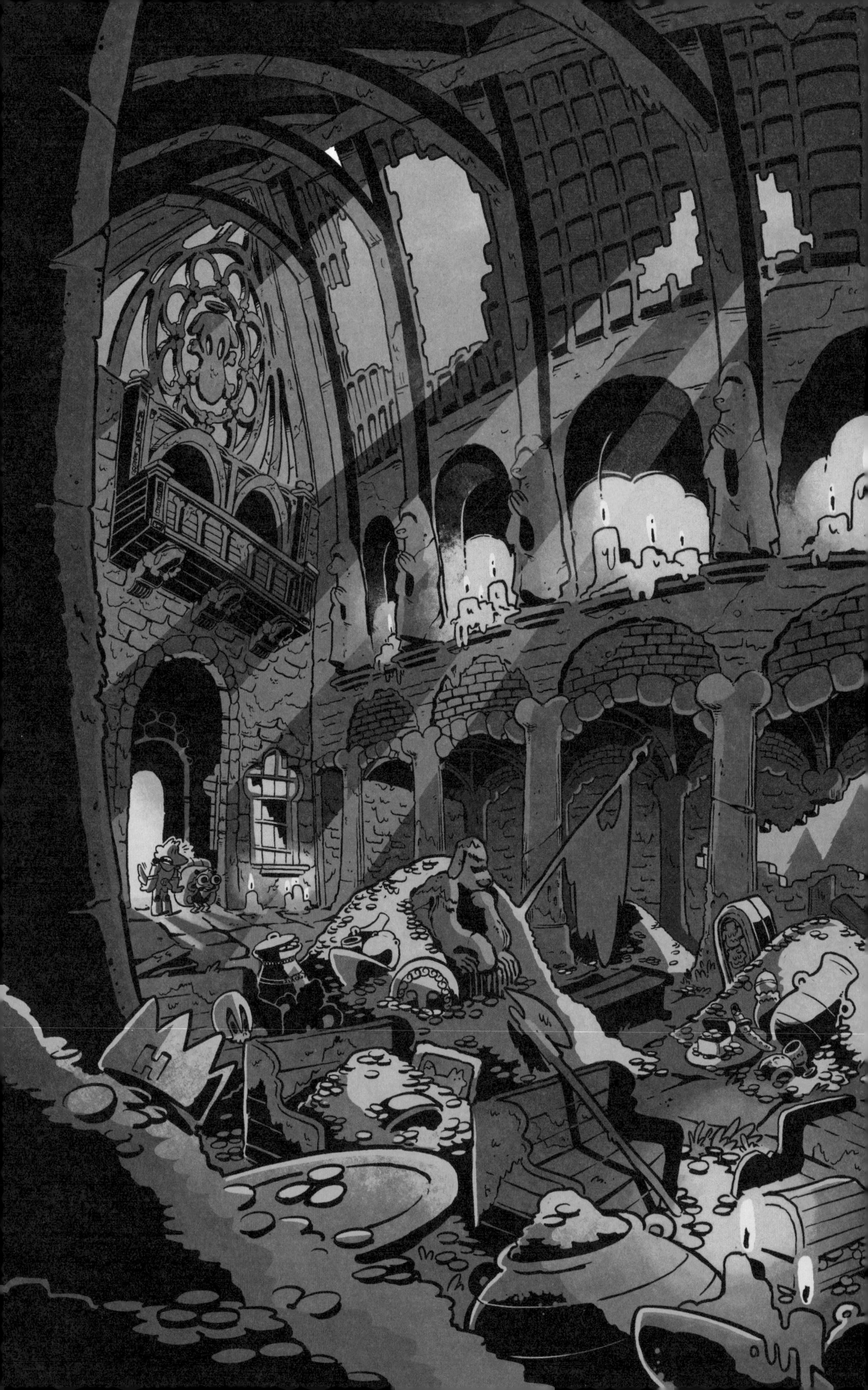

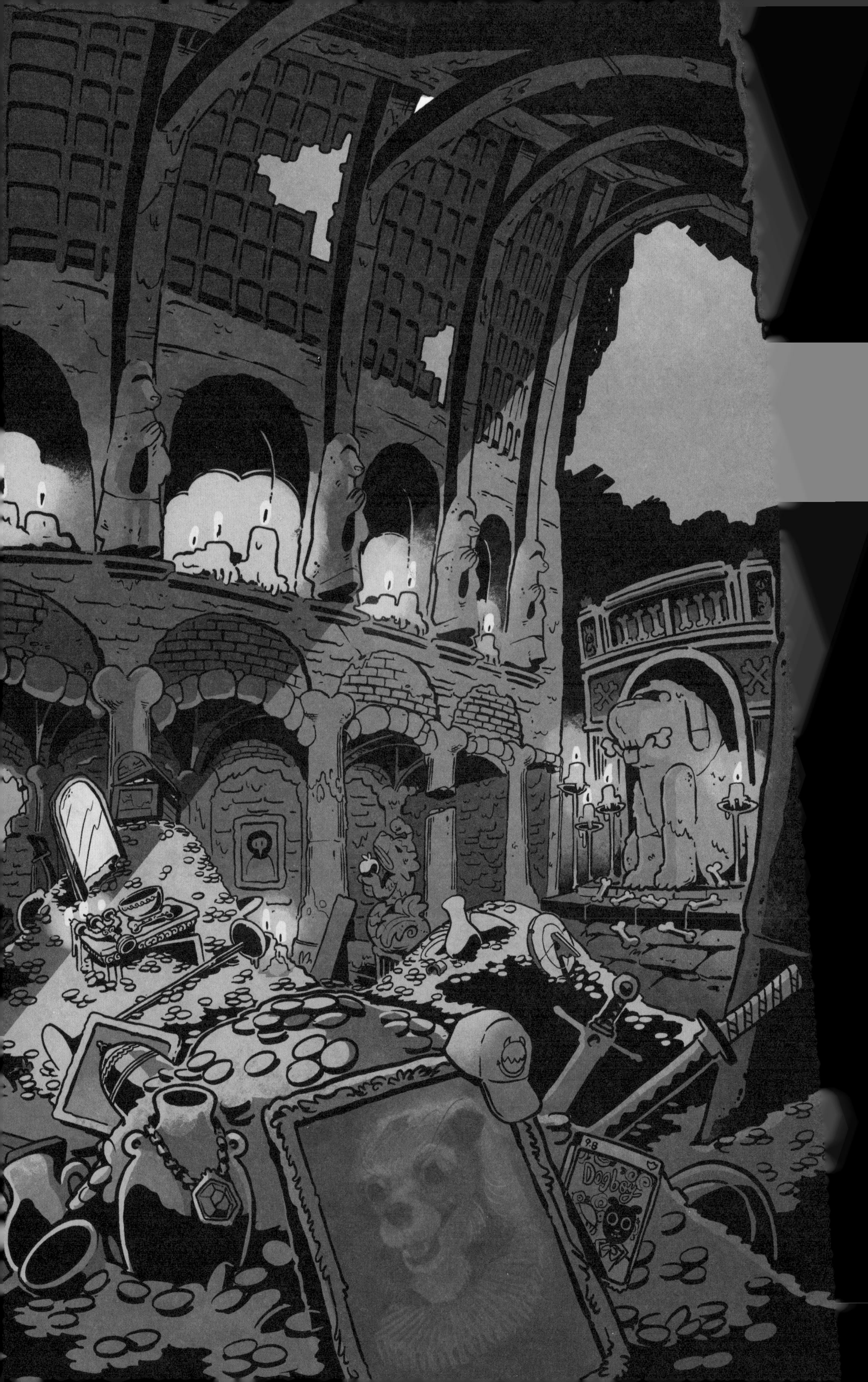
9.8
Dogboy

WOW! THE FARMER WAS TELLING THE TRUTH!

SO MUCH...

I WAS PRETTY SURE HE WAS GOING TO TRY AND MURDER US!

S-SO MUCH GOLD!

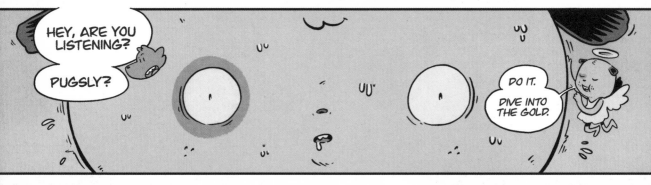

HEY, ARE YOU LISTENING?

PUGSLY?

DO IT. DIVE INTO THE GOLD.

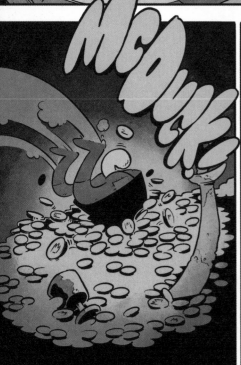

MCDUNK!

RUSTLE RUSTLE RUSTLE

I'M RICH!

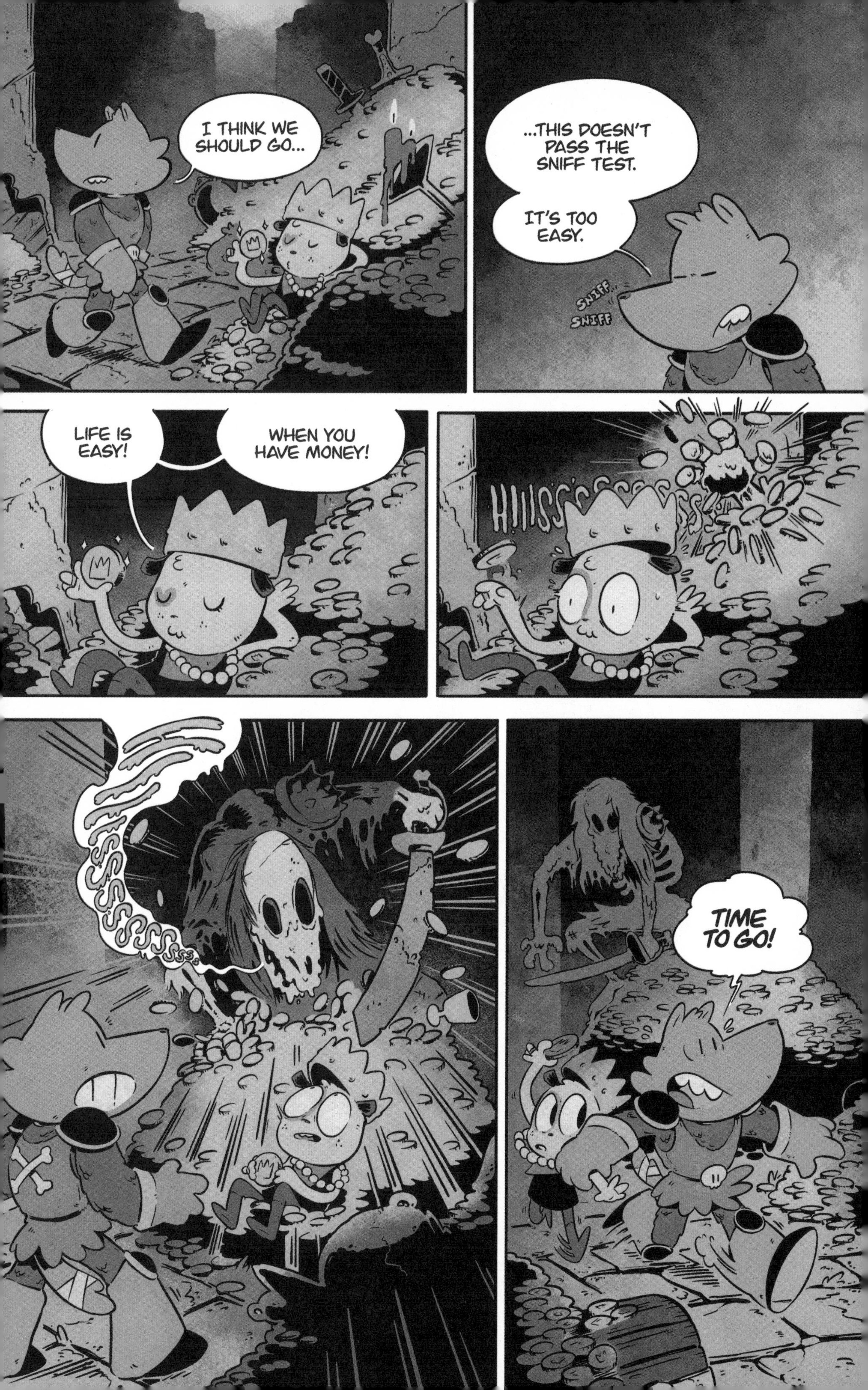
I THINK WE SHOULD GO...
...THIS DOESN'T PASS THE SNIFF TEST.
IT'S TOO EASY.
SNIFF
SNIFF
LIFE IS EASY!
WHEN YOU HAVE MONEY!
HIISSSSSSSS
TIME TO GO!

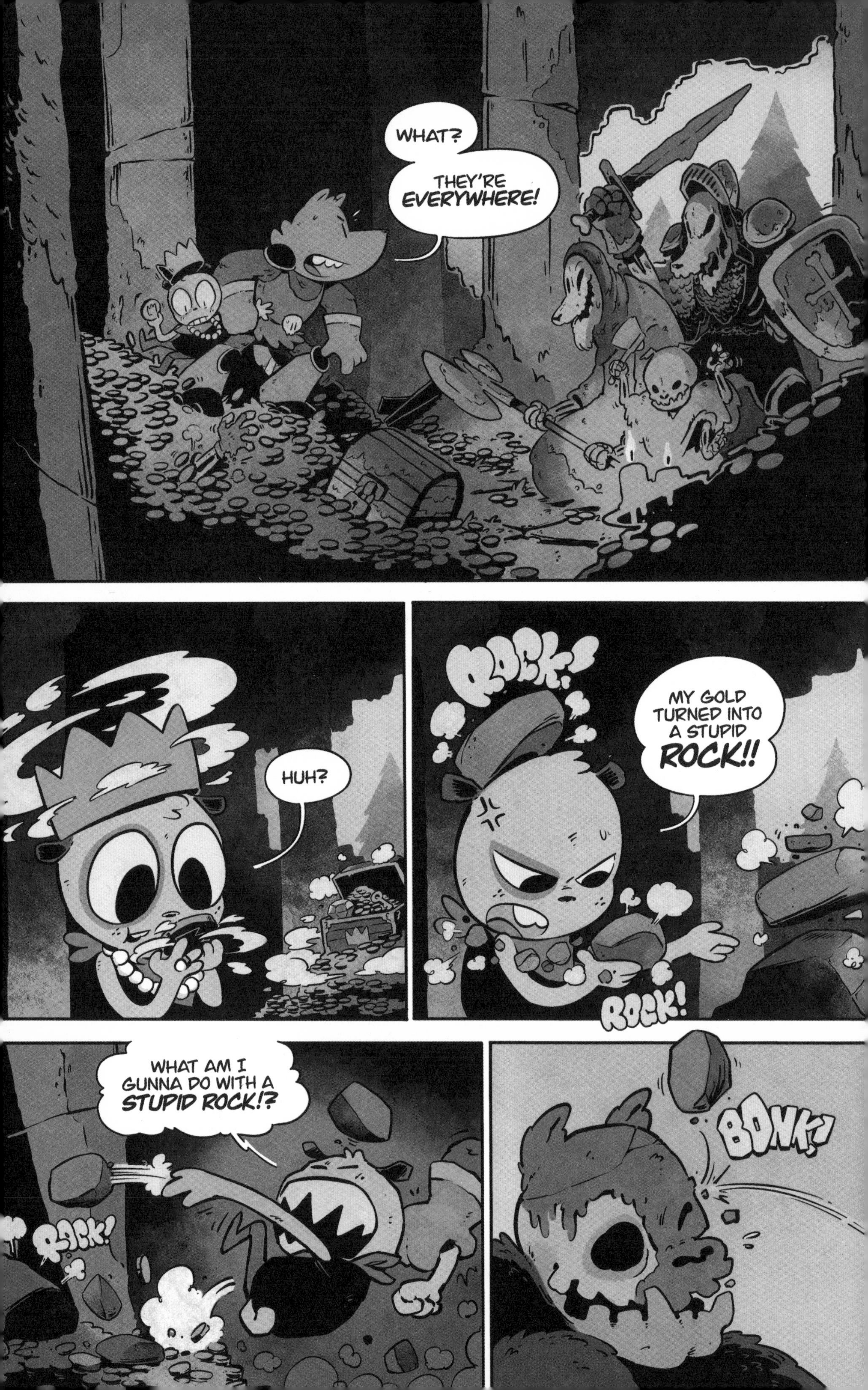
WHAT?
THEY'RE EVERYWHERE!
HUH?
ROCK!
MY GOLD TURNED INTO A STUPID ROCK!!
ROCK!
WHAT AM I GUNNA DO WITH A STUPID ROCK!?
ROCK!
BONK!

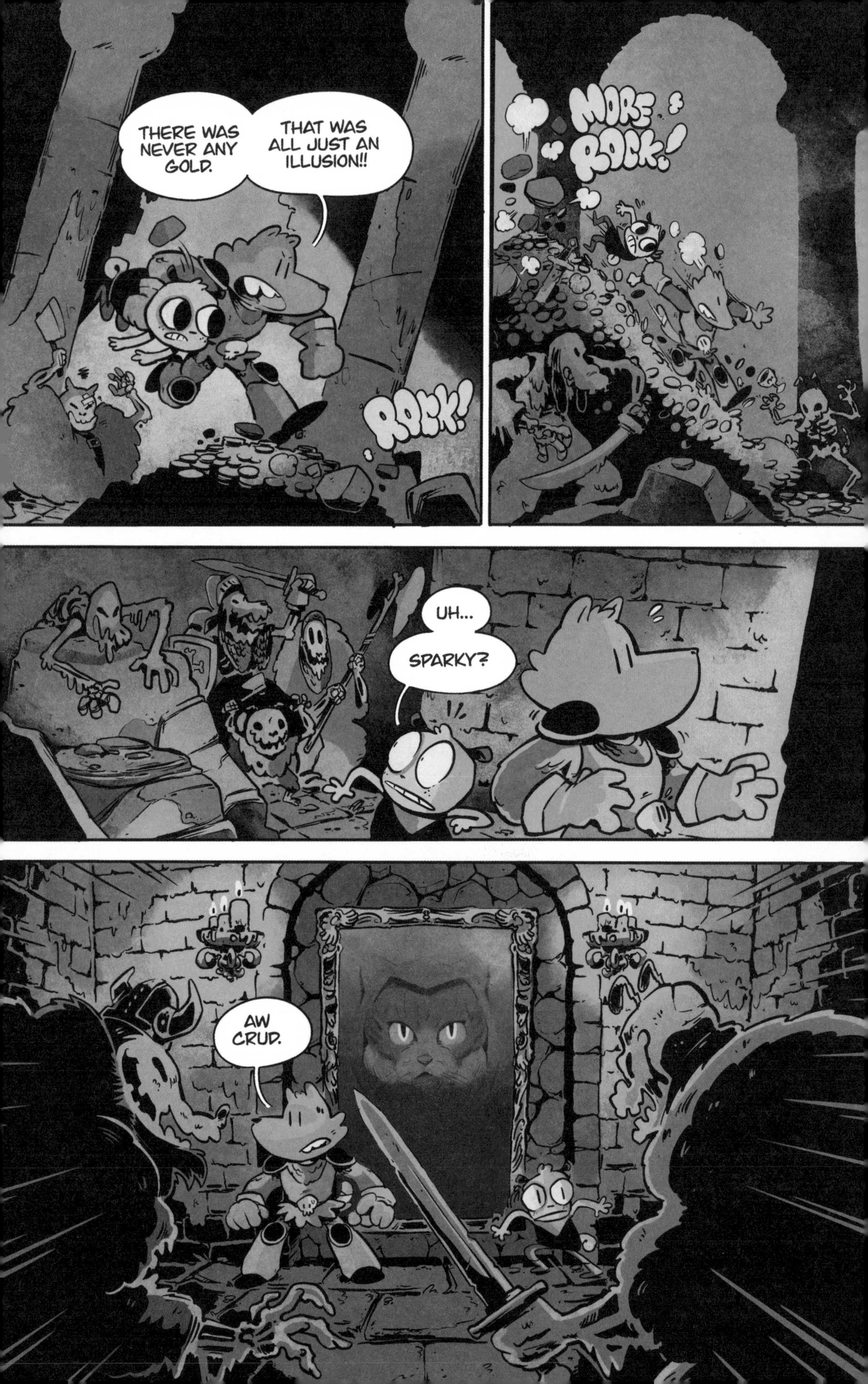
THERE WAS NEVER ANY GOLD.
THAT WAS ALL JUST AN ILLUSION!!
ROCK!
MORE ROCK!
UH...
SPARKY?
AW CRUD.

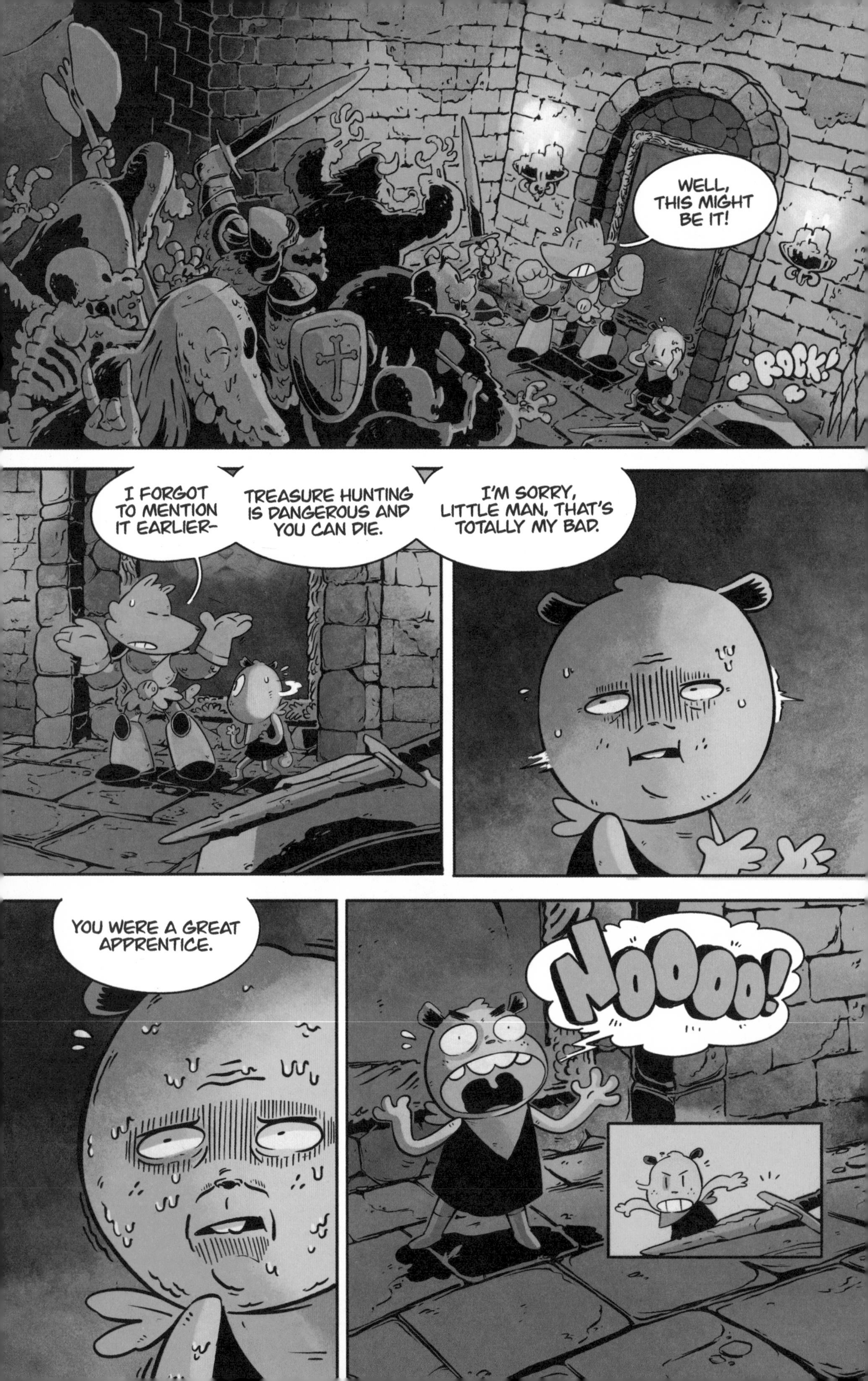
WELL, THIS MIGHT BE IT!
ROCK!
I FORGOT TO MENTION IT EARLIER-
TREASURE HUNTING IS DANGEROUS AND YOU CAN DIE.
I'M SORRY, LITTLE MAN, THAT'S TOTALLY MY BAD.
YOU WERE A GREAT APPRENTICE.
NOOOOO!

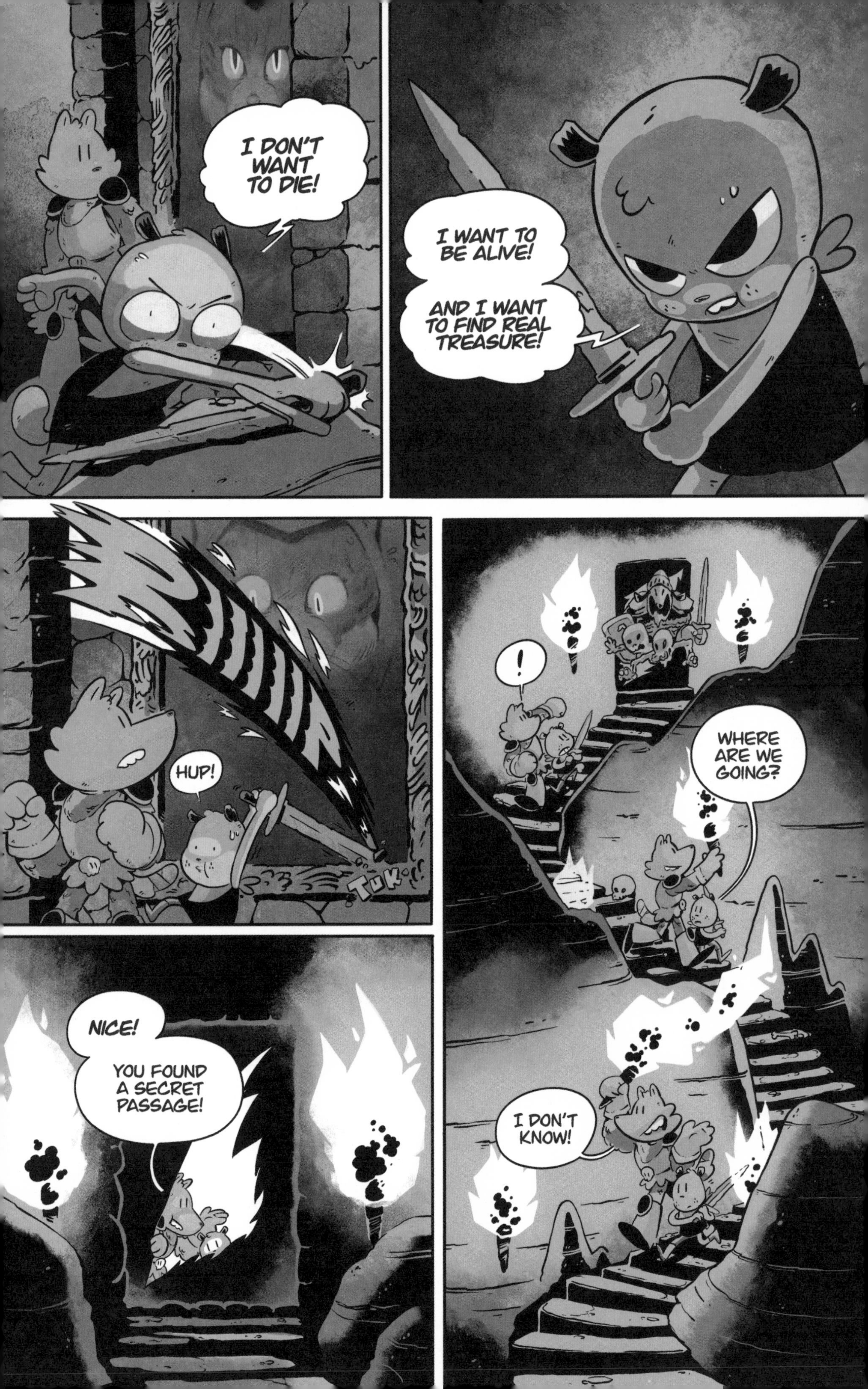
I DON'T WANT TO DIE!
I WANT TO BE ALIVE!
AND I WANT TO FIND REAL TREASURE!
HUP!
TUK
!
WHERE ARE WE GOING?
I DON'T KNOW!
NICE!
YOU FOUND A SECRET PASSAGE!

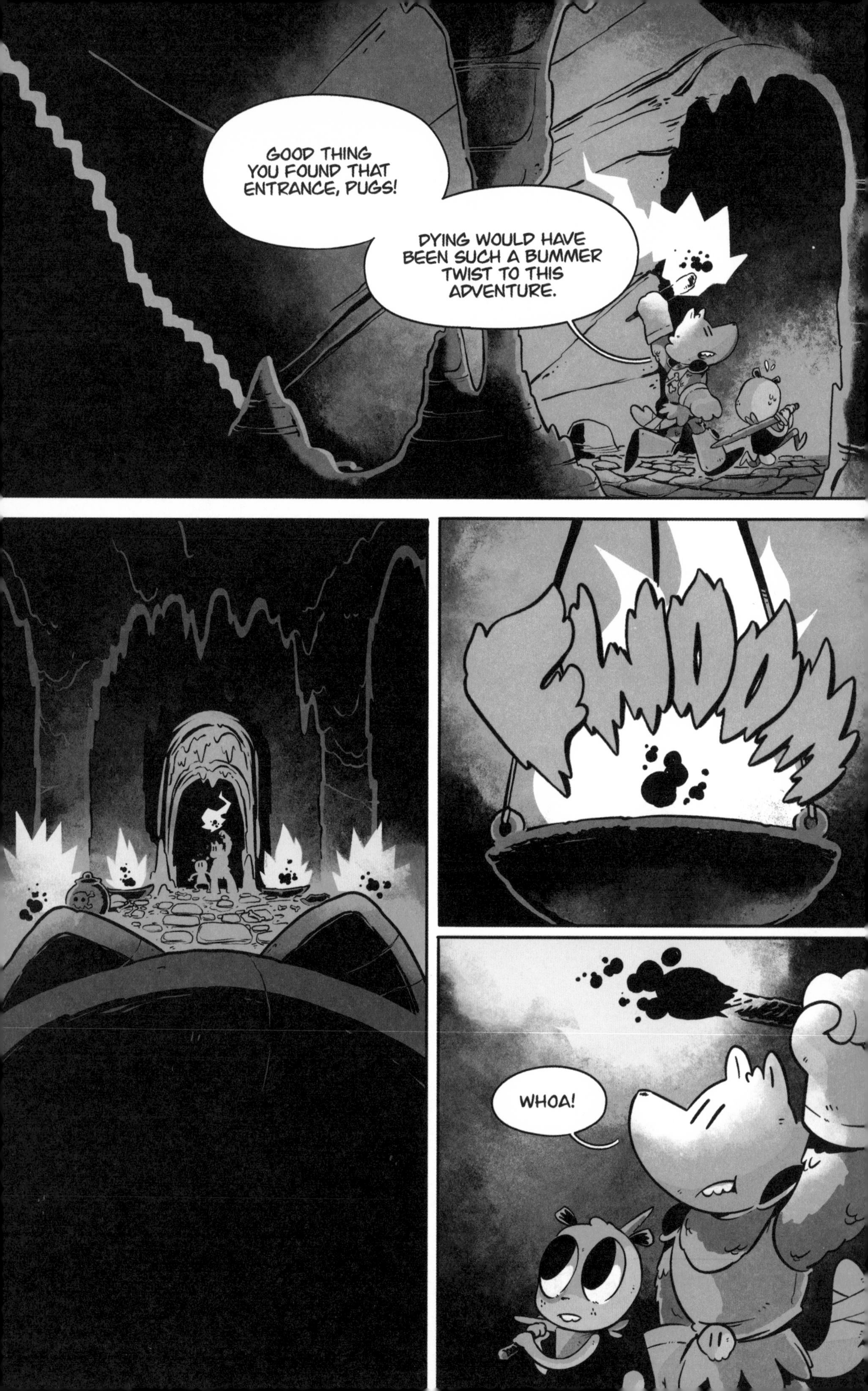
GOOD THING YOU FOUND THAT ENTRANCE, PUGS!
DYING WOULD HAVE BEEN SUCH A BUMMER TWIST TO THIS ADVENTURE.
FWOOM
WHOA!

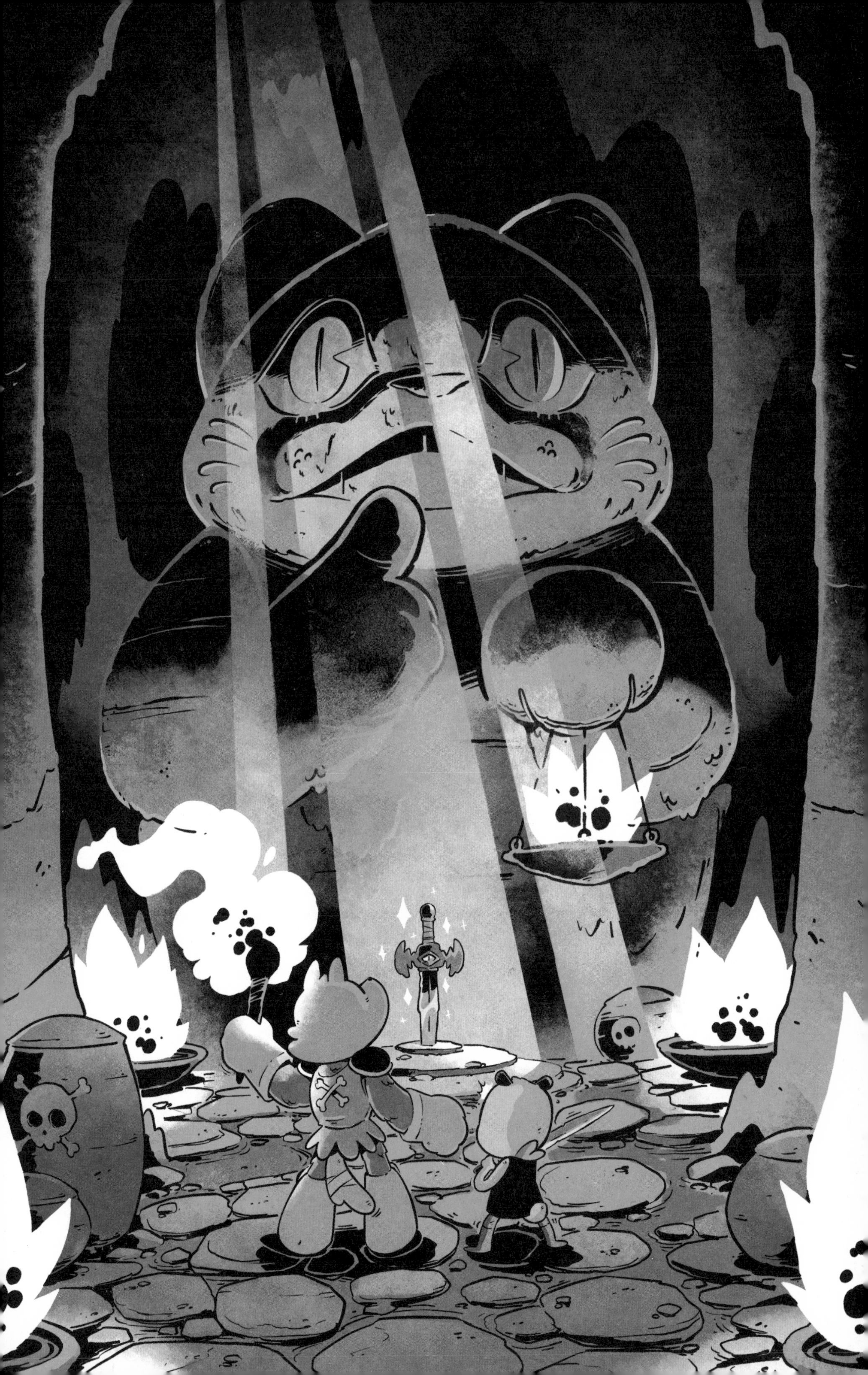

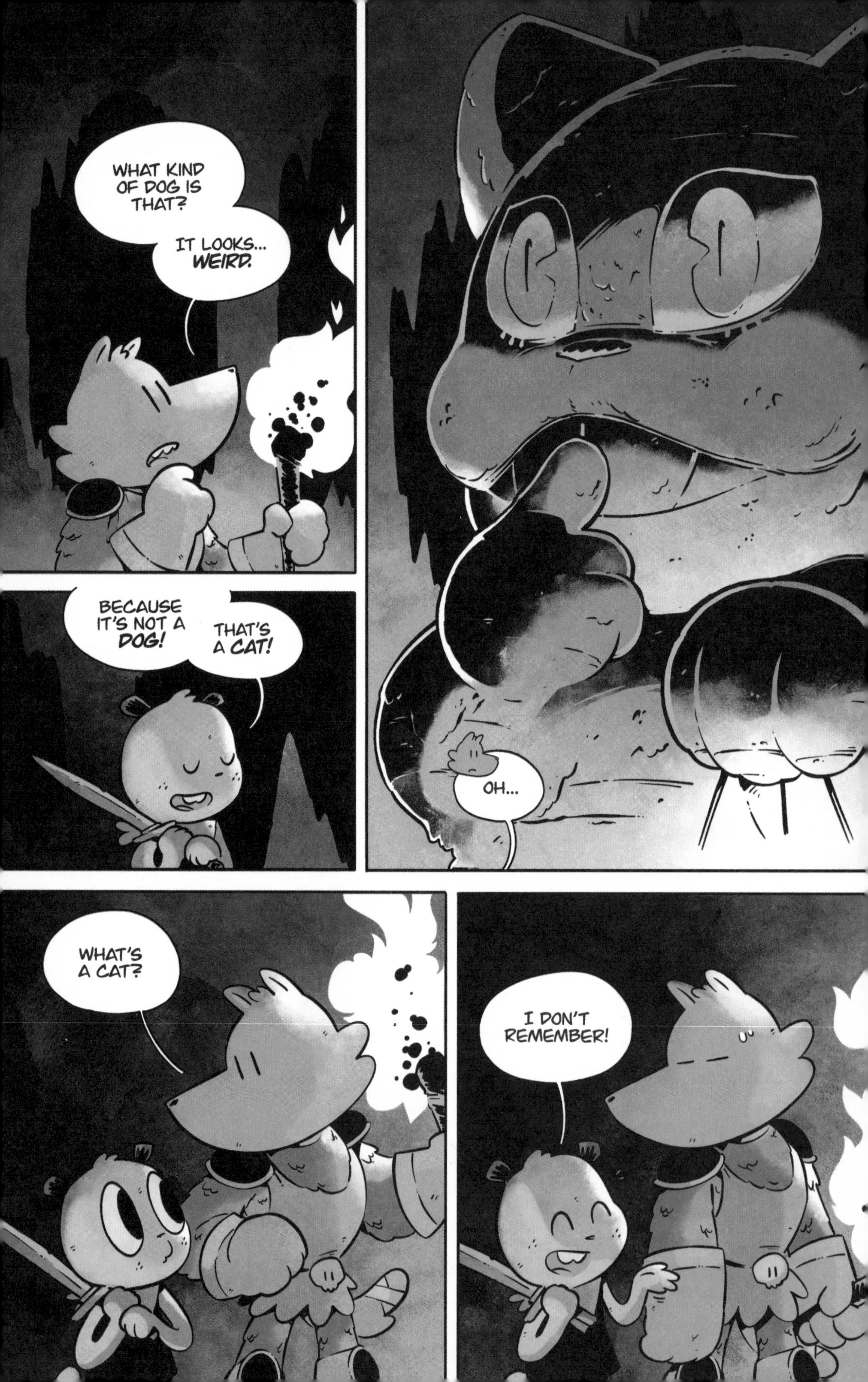
WHAT KIND OF DOG IS THAT?
IT LOOKS... WEIRD.
BECAUSE IT'S NOT A DOG!
THAT'S A CAT!
OH...
WHAT'S A CAT?
I DON'T REMEMBER!

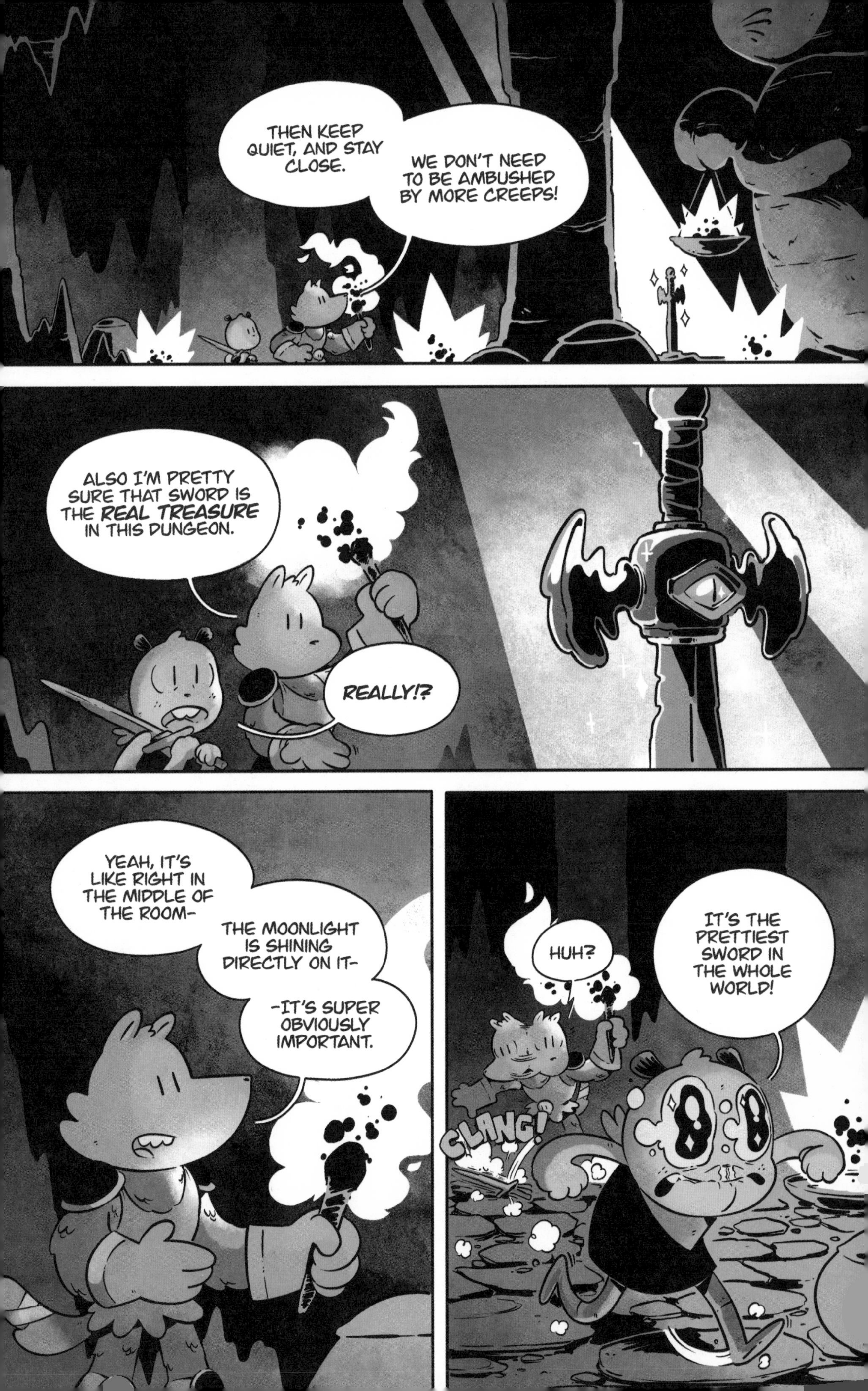
THEN KEEP QUIET, AND STAY CLOSE.
WE DON'T NEED TO BE AMBUSHED BY MORE CREEPS!
ALSO I'M PRETTY SURE THAT SWORD IS THE REAL TREASURE IN THIS DUNGEON.
REALLY!?
YEAH, IT'S LIKE RIGHT IN THE MIDDLE OF THE ROOM-
THE MOONLIGHT IS SHINING DIRECTLY ON IT-
-IT'S SUPER OBVIOUSLY IMPORTANT.
HUH?
IT'S THE PRETTIEST SWORD IN THE WHOLE WORLD!
CLANG!

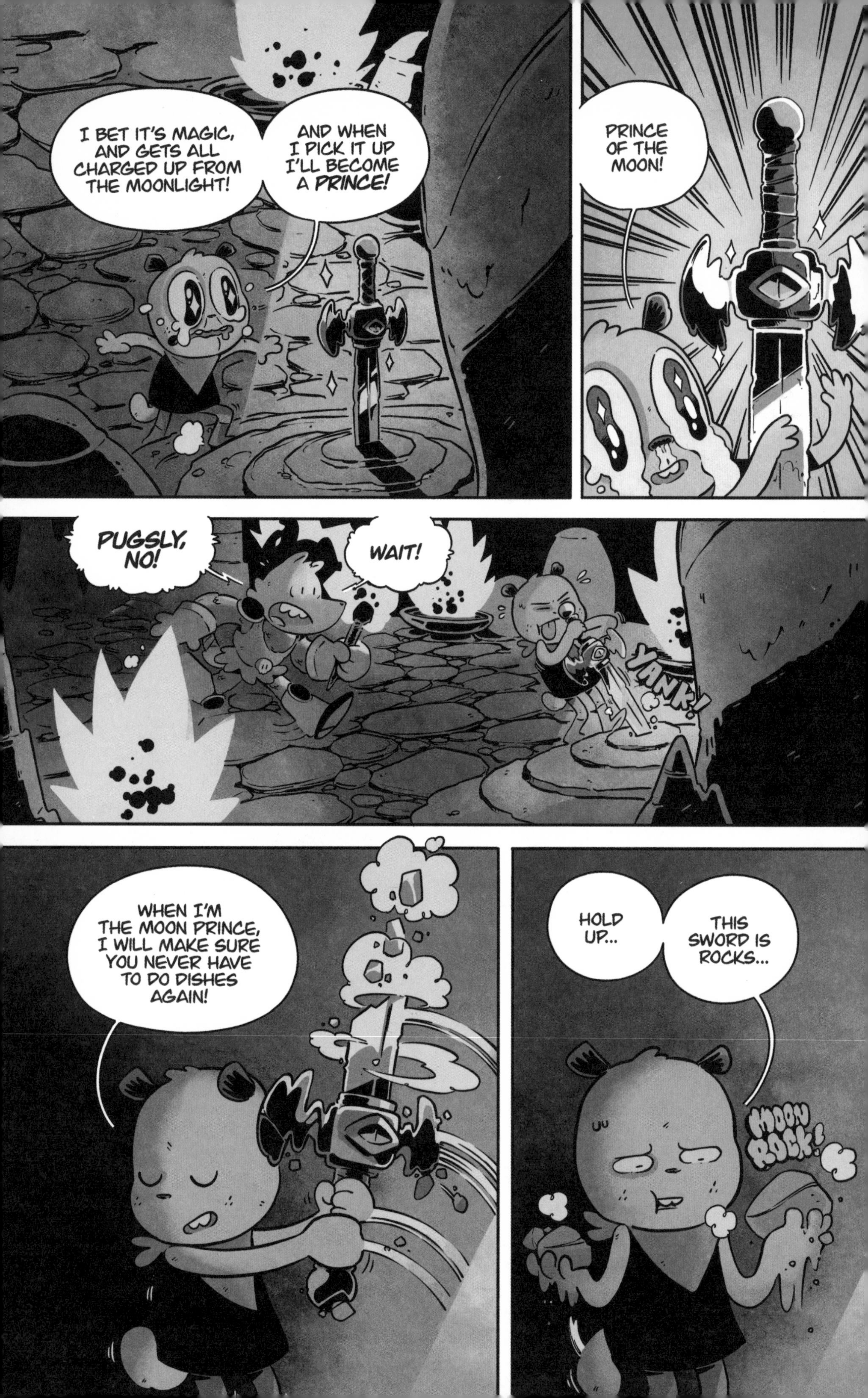
I BET IT'S MAGIC, AND GETS ALL CHARGED UP FROM THE MOONLIGHT!
AND WHEN I PICK IT UP I'LL BECOME A PRINCE!
PRINCE OF THE MOON!
PUGSLY, NO!
WAIT!
YANK!
WHEN I'M THE MOON PRINCE, I WILL MAKE SURE YOU NEVER HAVE TO DO DISHES AGAIN!
HOLD UP...
THIS SWORD IS ROCKS...
MOON ROCK!

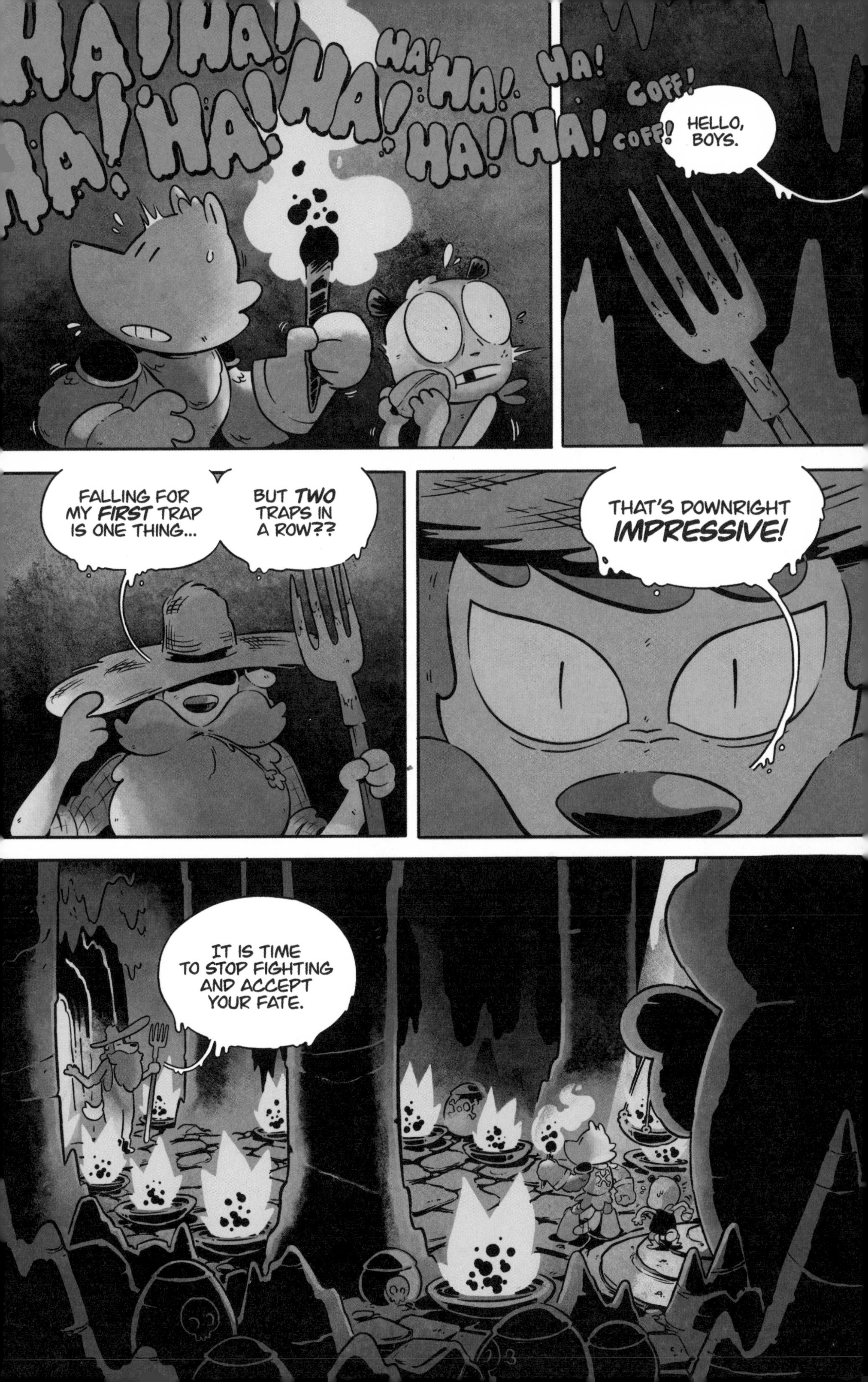
HA! HA! HA! HA! HA! HA! HA! HA! HA! HA!
COFF! COFF!
HELLO, BOYS.
FALLING FOR MY FIRST TRAP IS ONE THING...
BUT TWO TRAPS IN A ROW??
THAT'S DOWNRIGHT IMPRESSIVE!
IT IS TIME TO STOP FIGHTING AND ACCEPT YOUR FATE.

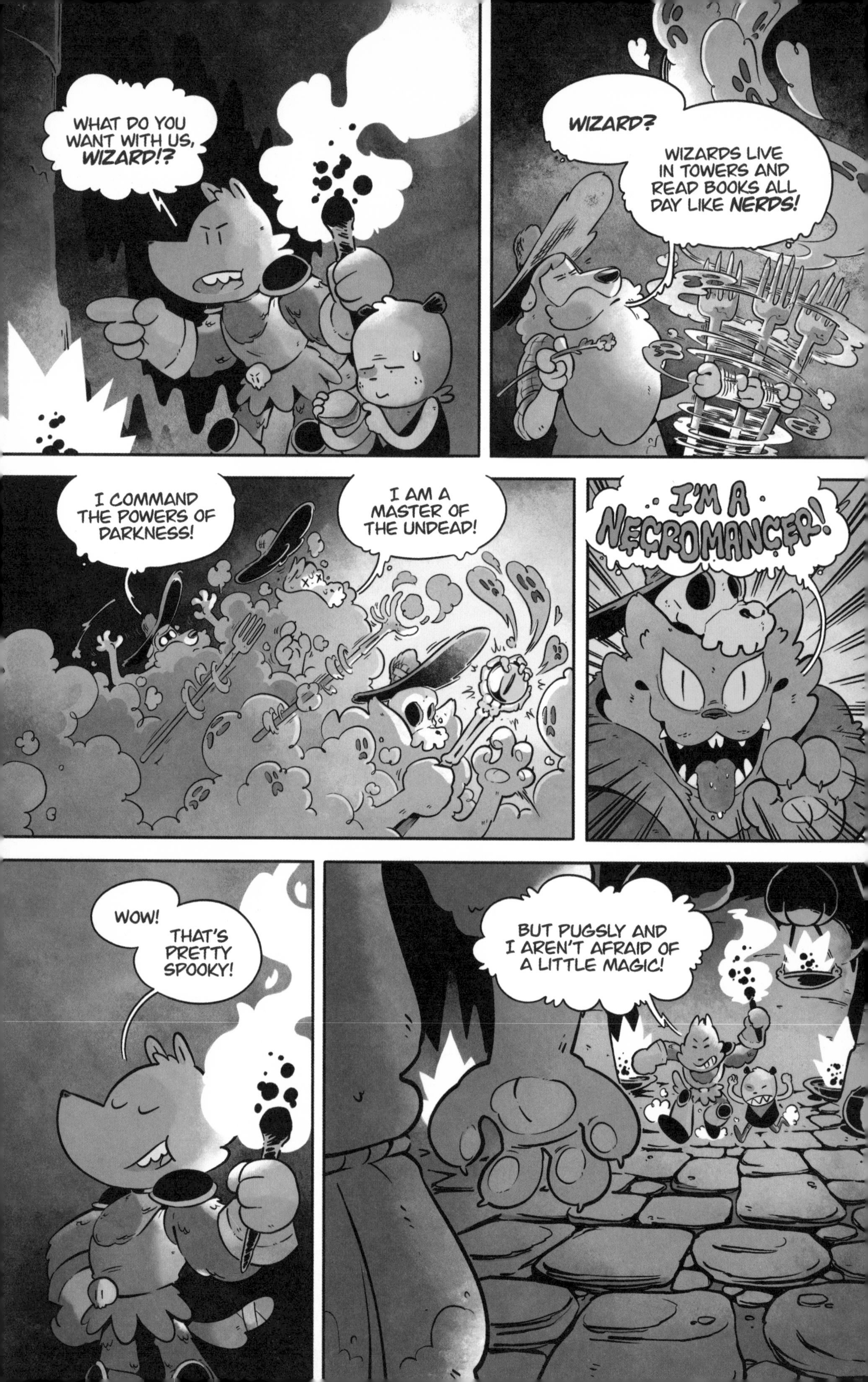
WHAT DO YOU WANT WITH US, WIZARD!?
WIZARD?
WIZARDS LIVE IN TOWERS AND READ BOOKS ALL DAY LIKE NERDS!
I COMMAND THE POWERS OF DARKNESS!
I AM A MASTER OF THE UNDEAD!
I'M A NECROMANCER!
WOW!
THAT'S PRETTY SPOOKY!
BUT PUGSLY AND I AREN'T AFRAID OF A LITTLE MAGIC!

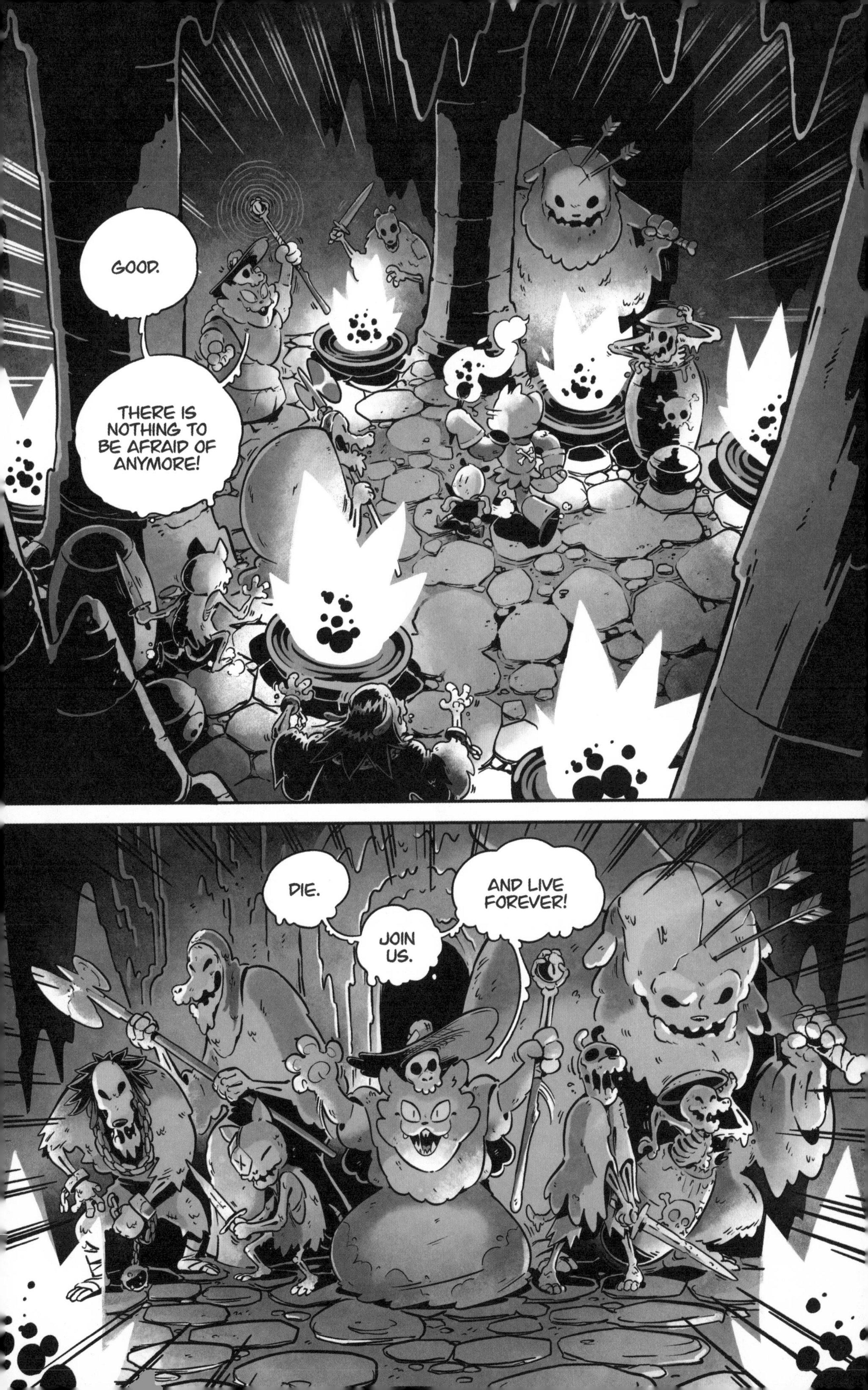
GOOD.
THERE IS NOTHING TO BE AFRAID OF ANYMORE!
DIE.
JOIN US.
AND LIVE FOREVER!

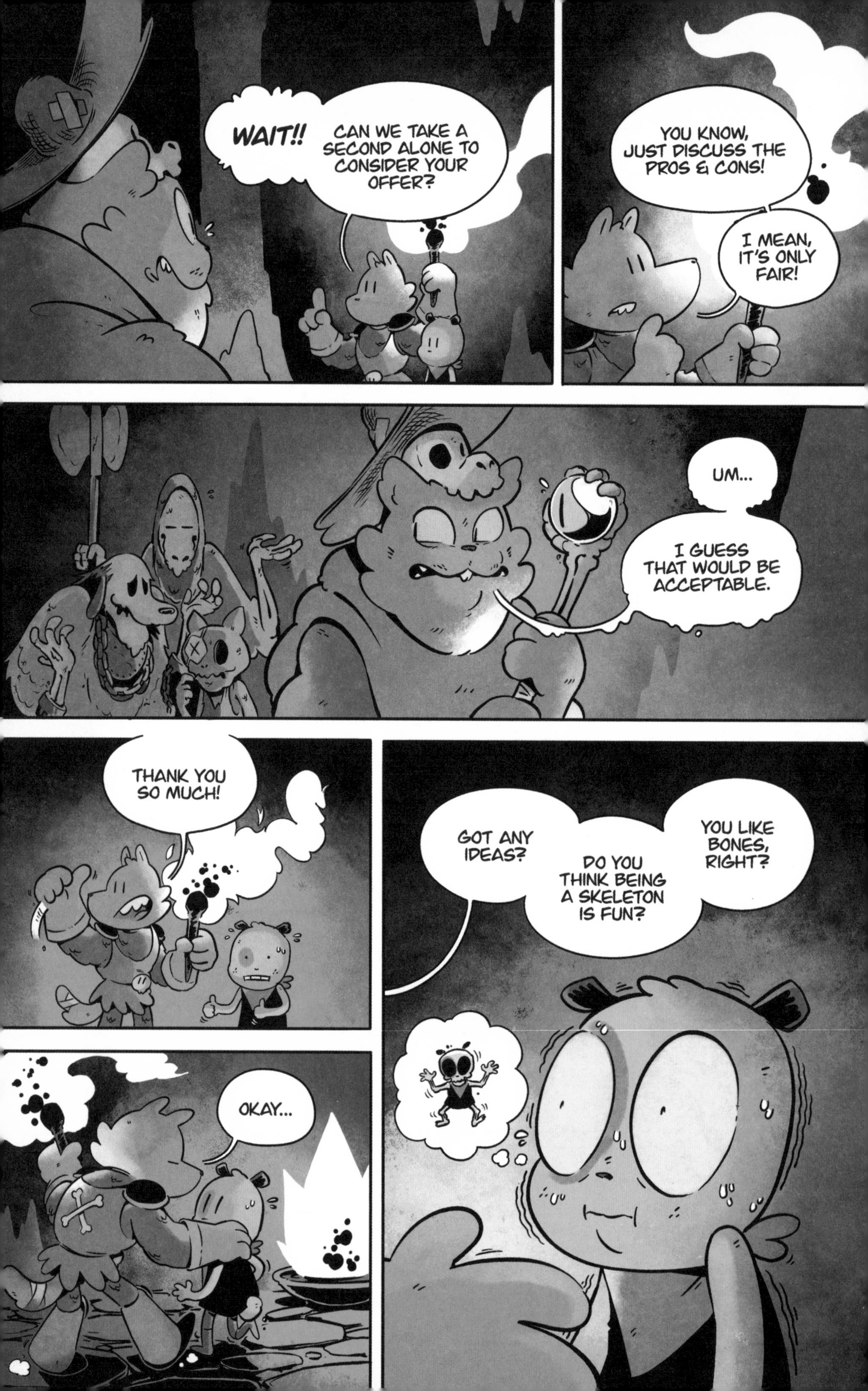
WAIT!!
CAN WE TAKE A SECOND ALONE TO CONSIDER YOUR OFFER?
YOU KNOW, JUST DISCUSS THE PROS & CONS!
I MEAN, IT'S ONLY FAIR!
UM...
I GUESS THAT WOULD BE ACCEPTABLE.
THANK YOU SO MUCH!
OKAY...
GOT ANY IDEAS?
DO YOU THINK BEING A SKELETON IS FUN?
YOU LIKE BONES, RIGHT?

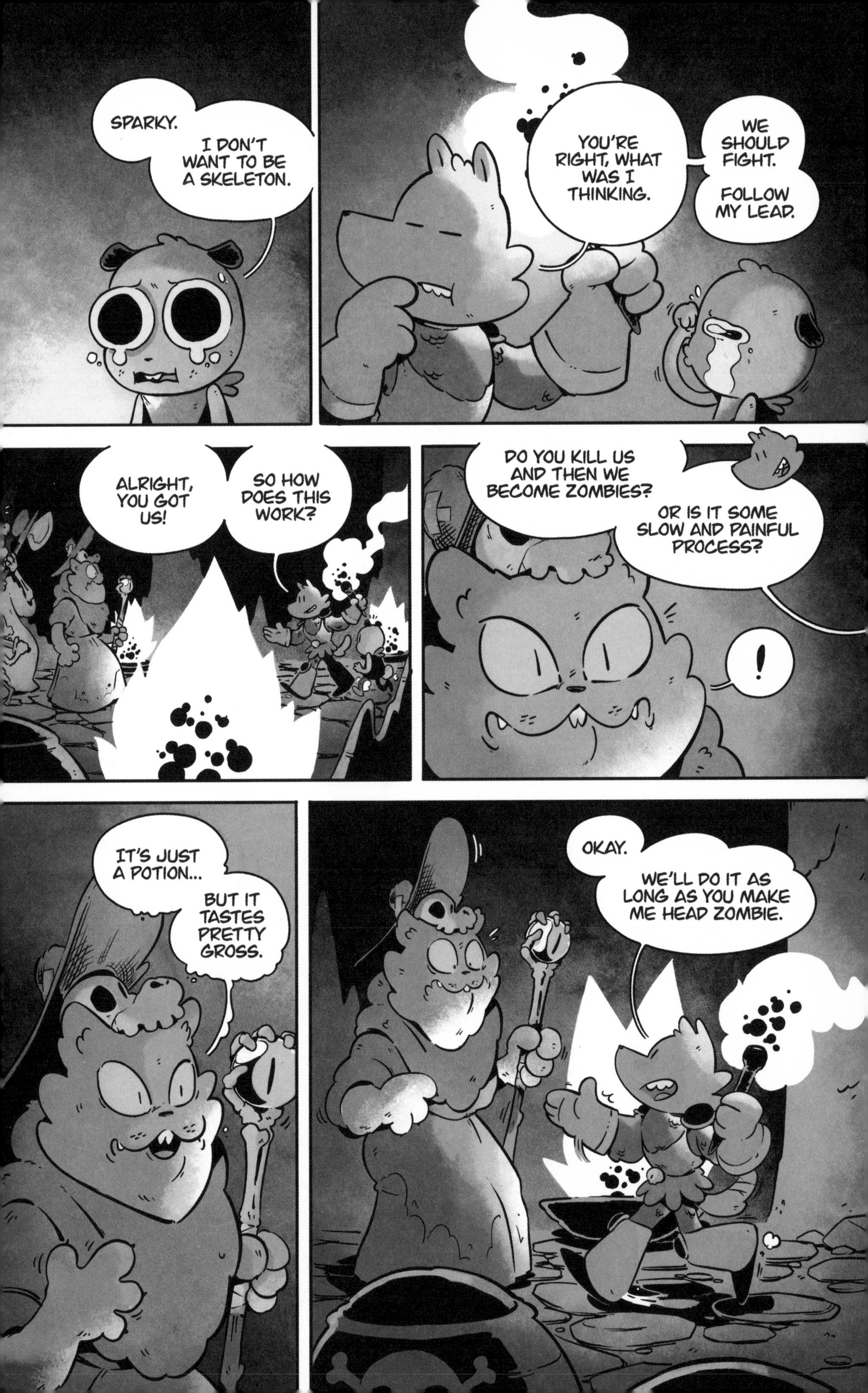
SPARKY.
I DON'T WANT TO BE A SKELETON.
YOU'RE RIGHT, WHAT WAS I THINKING.
WE SHOULD FIGHT.
FOLLOW MY LEAD.
ALRIGHT, YOU GOT US!
SO HOW DOES THIS WORK?
DO YOU KILL US AND THEN WE BECOME ZOMBIES?
OR IS IT SOME SLOW AND PAINFUL PROCESS?
!
IT'S JUST A POTION...
BUT IT TASTES PRETTY GROSS.
OKAY.
WE'LL DO IT AS LONG AS YOU MAKE ME HEAD ZOMBIE.

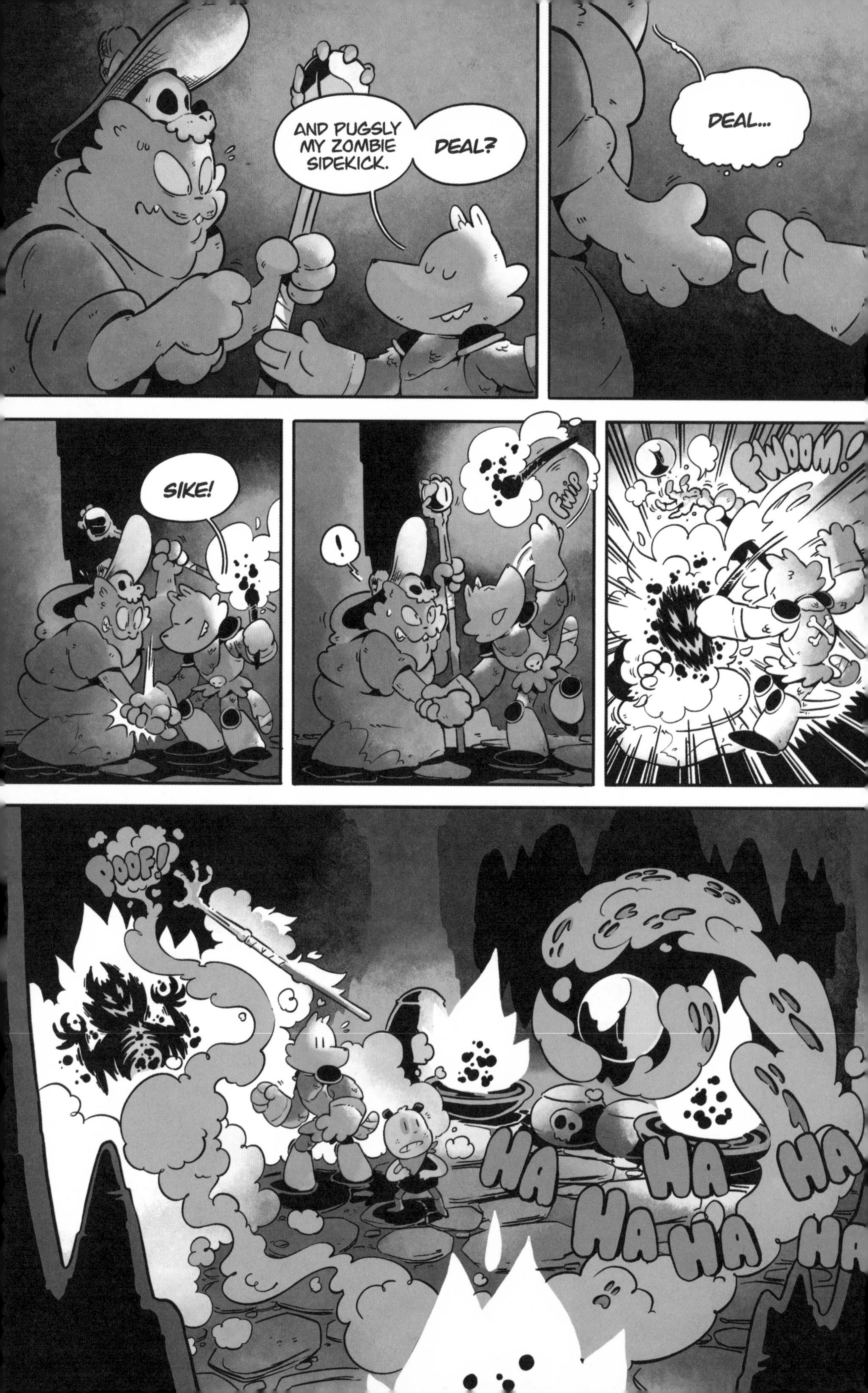
AND PUGSLY MY ZOMBIE SIDEKICK.
DEAL?
DEAL...
SIKE!
!
FWIP
FWOOM!
POOF!
HA HA HA
HA HA HA HA

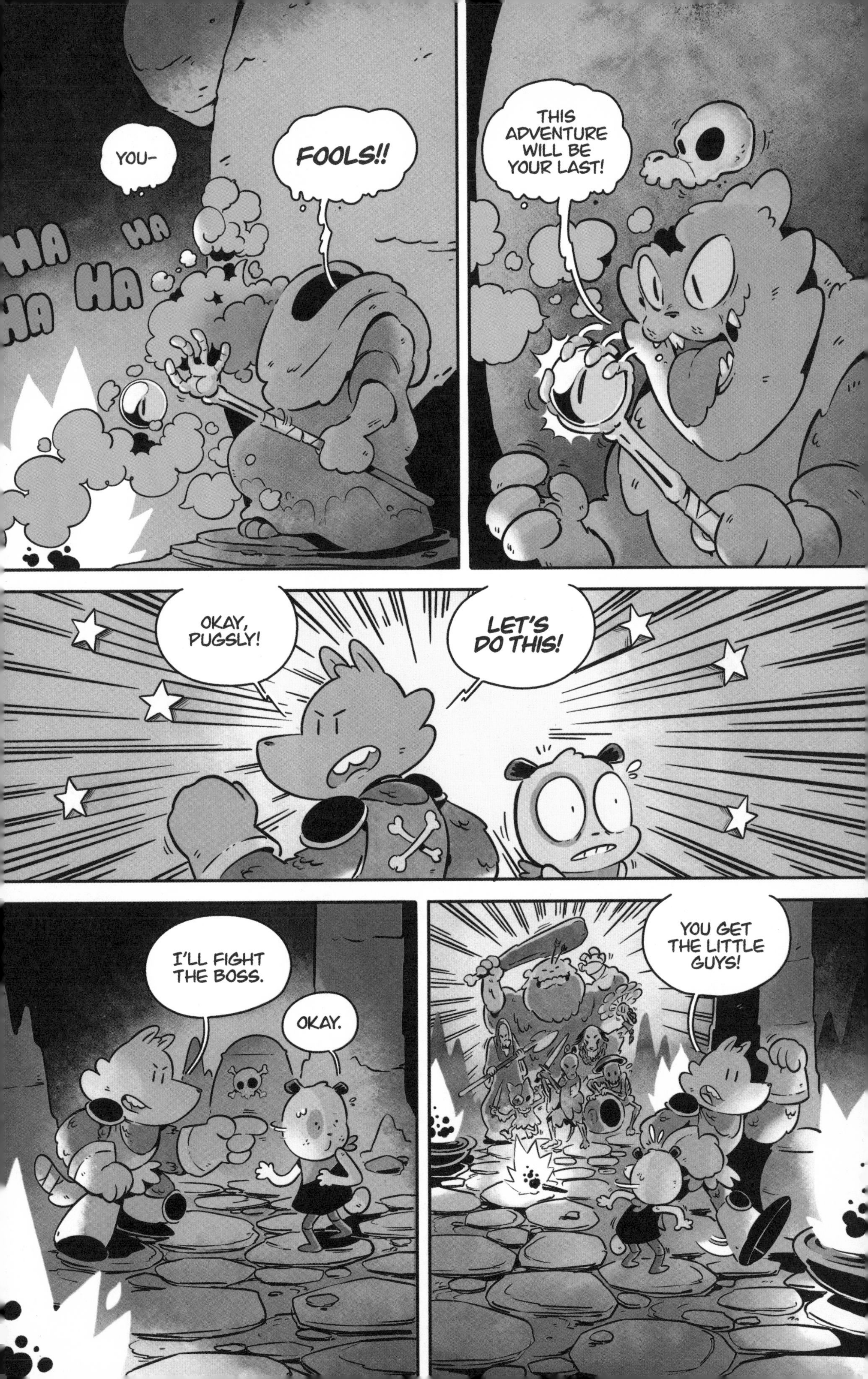
YOU-
FOOLS!!
HA
HA
HA
HA
THIS ADVENTURE WILL BE YOUR LAST!
OKAY, PUGSLY!
LET'S DO THIS!
I'LL FIGHT THE BOSS.
OKAY.
YOU GET THE LITTLE GUYS!

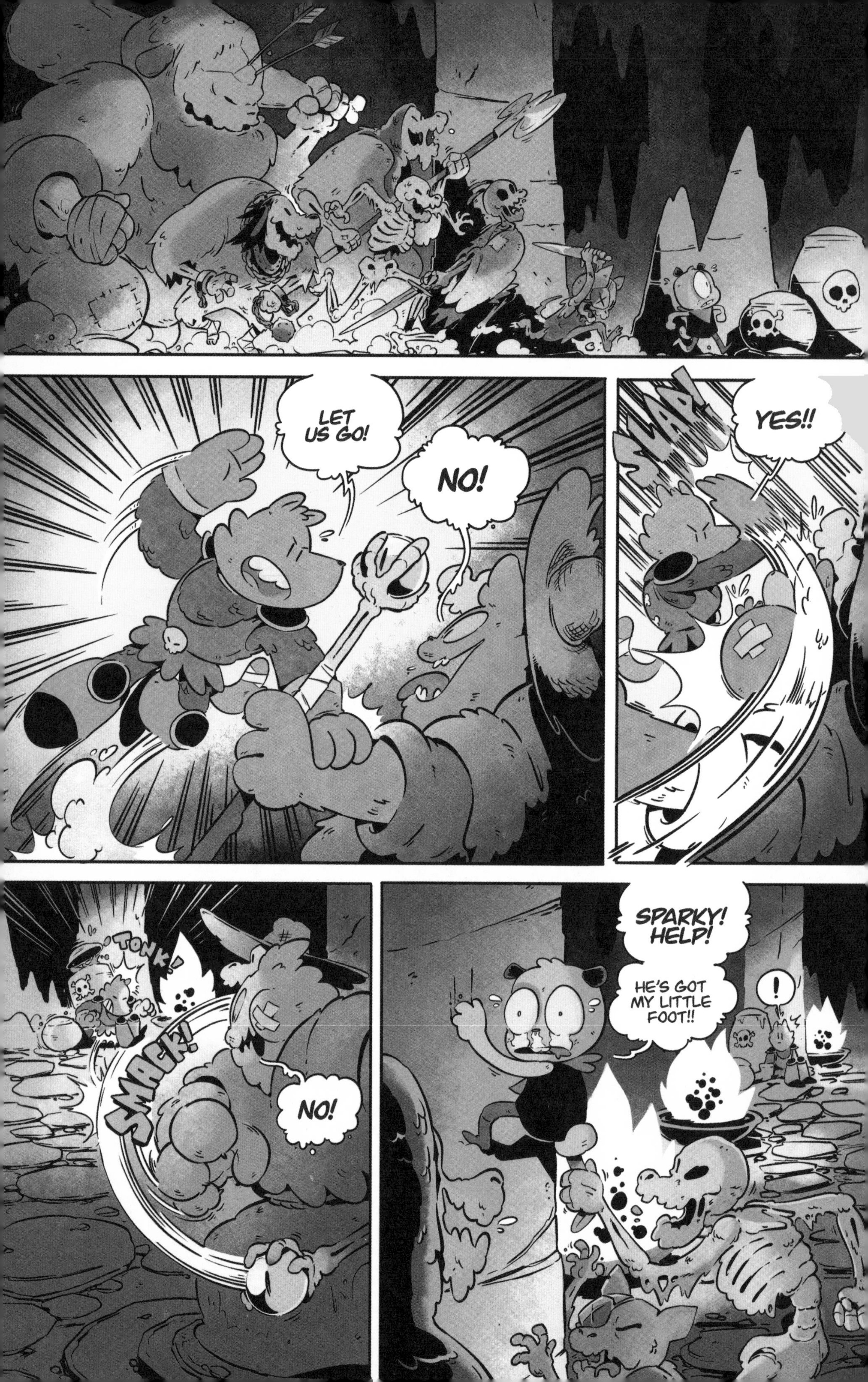
LET US GO!
NO!
YES!!
TONK!
SMACK!
NO!
SPARKY! HELP!
HE'S GOT MY LITTLE FOOT!!
!

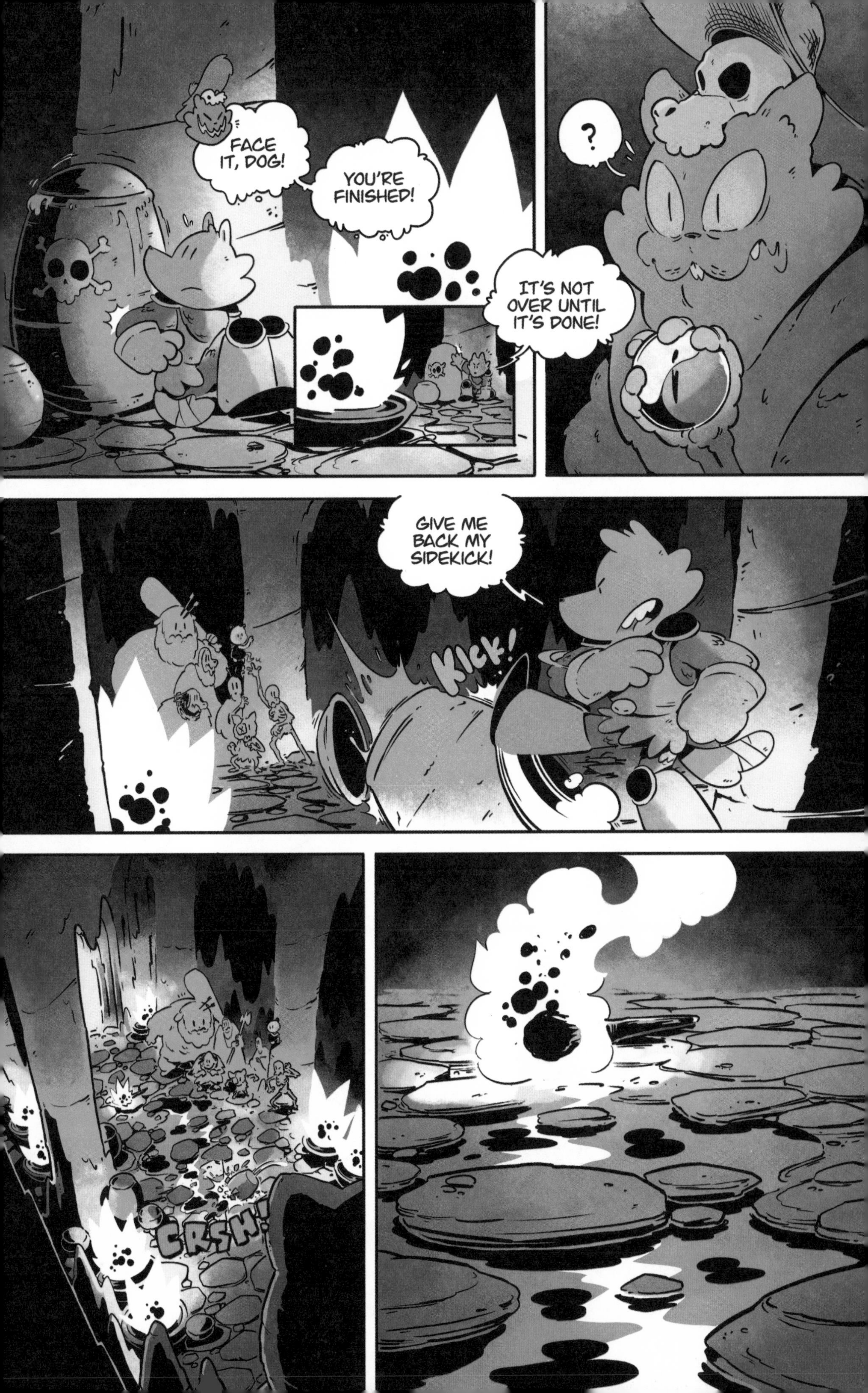
FACE IT, DOG!
YOU'RE FINISHED!
?
IT'S NOT OVER UNTIL IT'S DONE!
GIVE ME BACK MY SIDEKICK!
KICK!
CRSH!

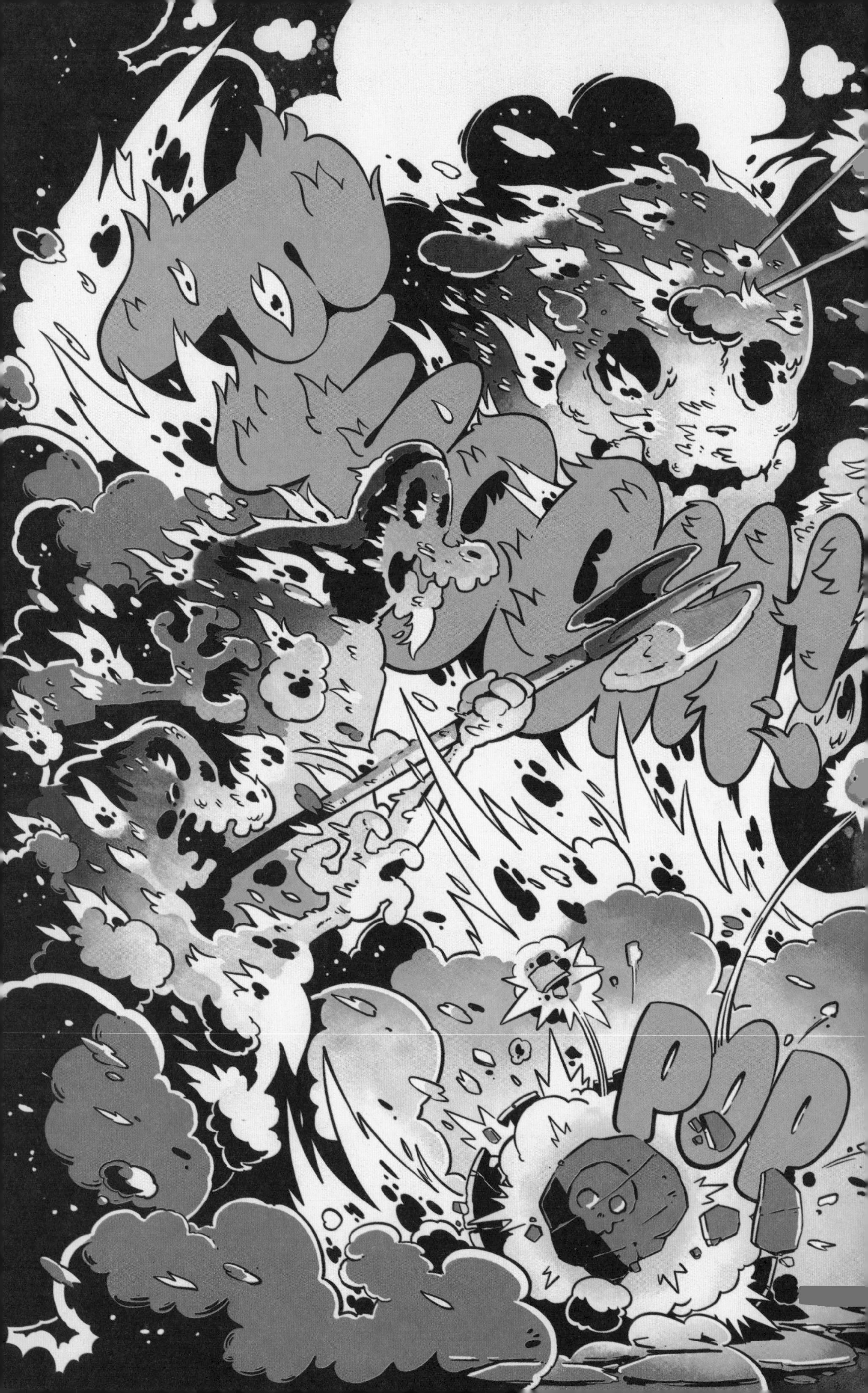
POP

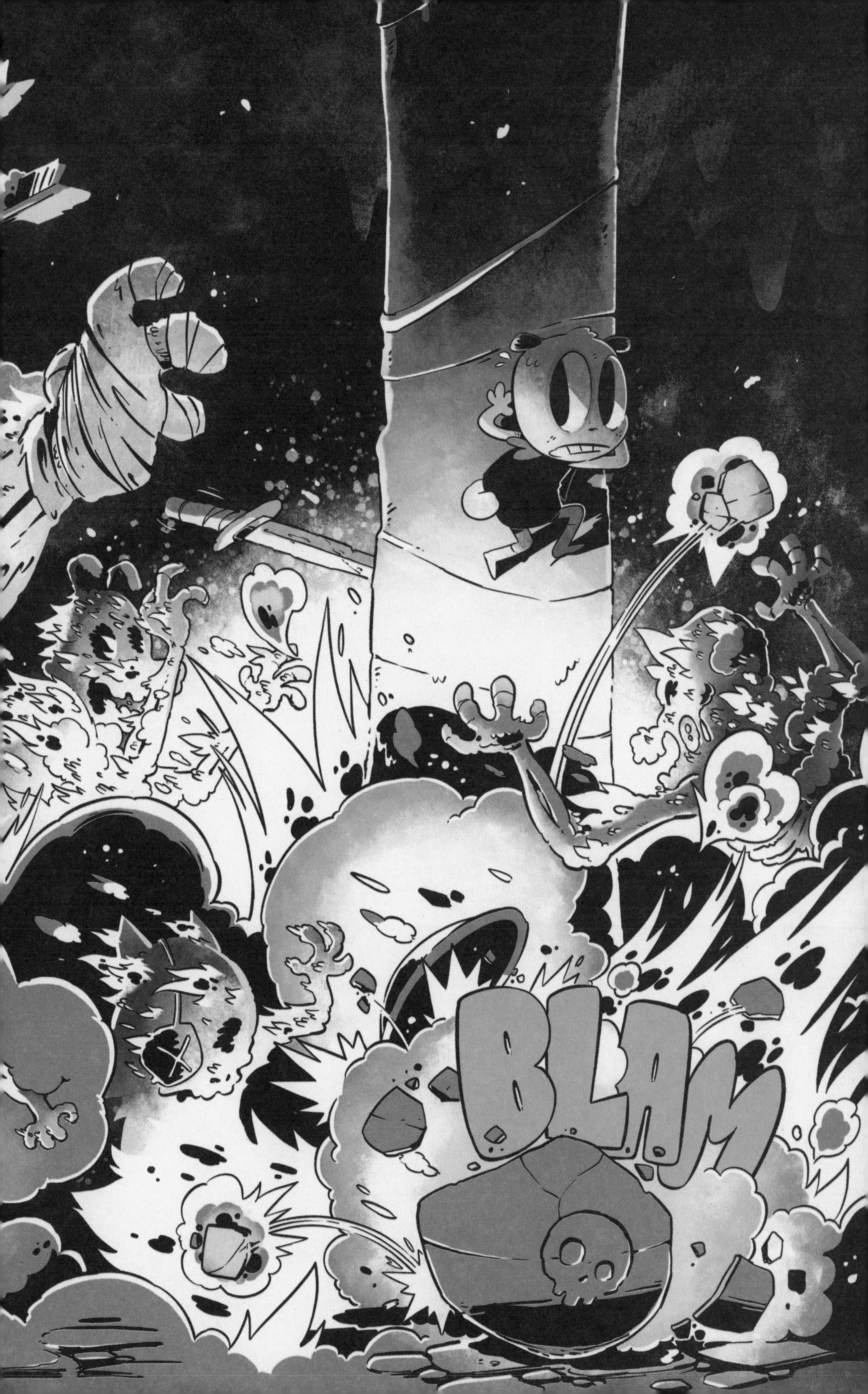
BLAM

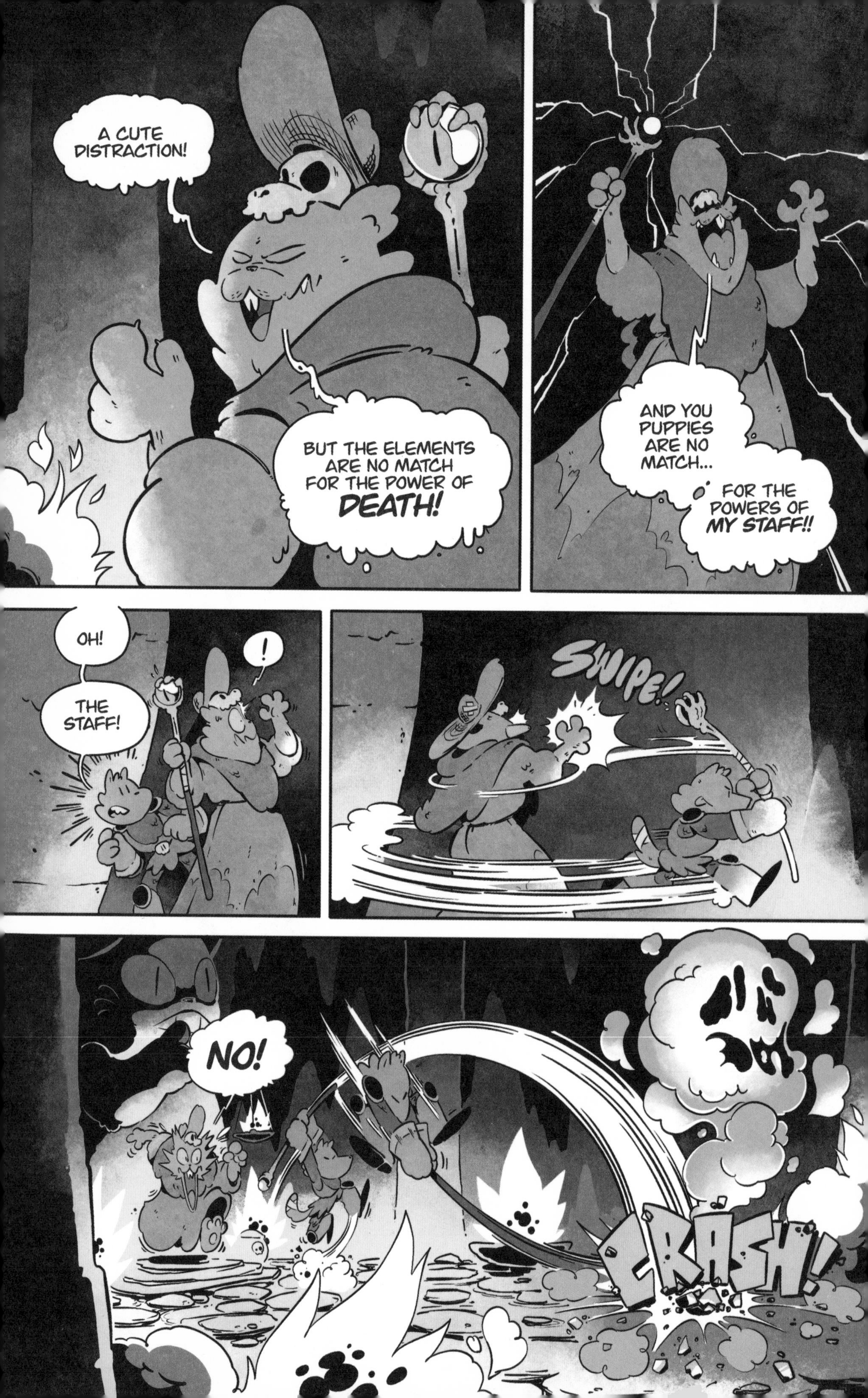
A CUTE DISTRACTION!
BUT THE ELEMENTS ARE NO MATCH FOR THE POWER OF DEATH!
AND YOU PUPPIES ARE NO MATCH...
FOR THE POWERS OF MY STAFF!!
OH!
THE STAFF!
!
SWIPE!
NO!
CRASH!

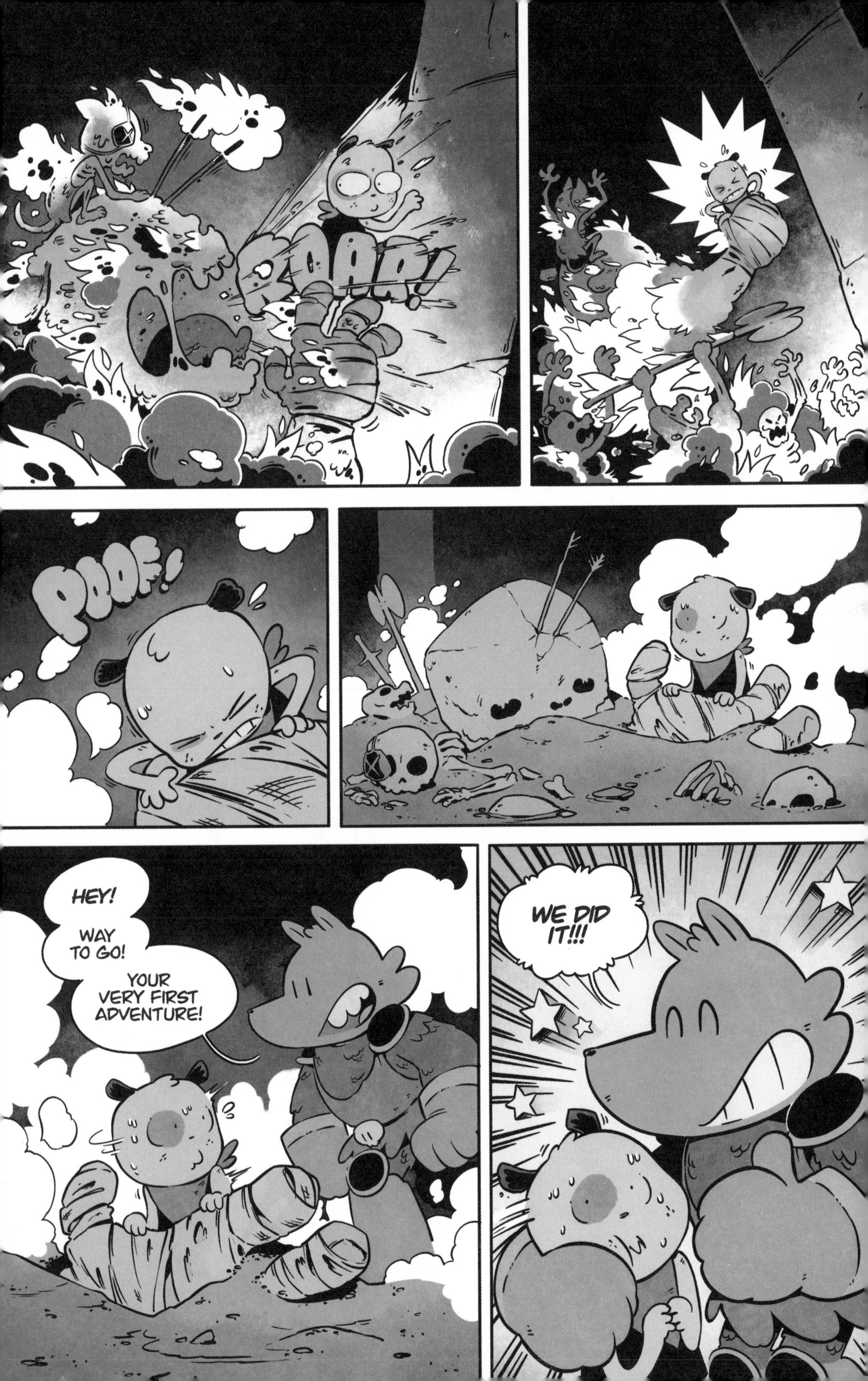
ROAR!
POOF!
HEY!
WAY TO GO!
YOUR VERY FIRST ADVENTURE!
WE DID IT!!!

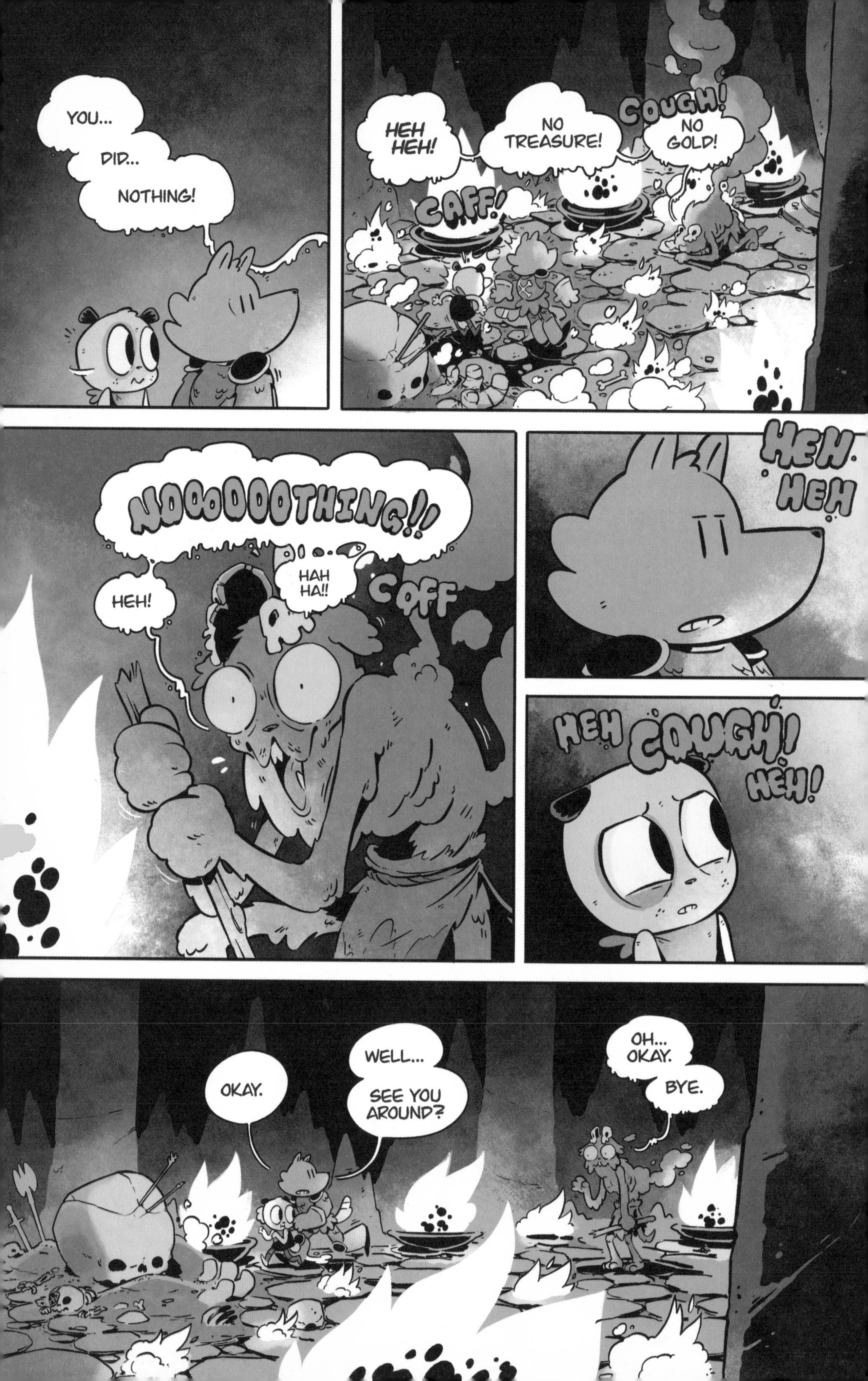
YOU...
DID...
NOTHING!
HEH HEH!
CAFF!
NO TREASURE!
COUGH!
NO GOLD!
NOOOOOOOTHING!!
HEH!
HAH HA!!
COFF
HEH. HEH
HEH
COUGH!
HEH!
OKAY.
WELL...
SEE YOU AROUND?
OH... OKAY.
BYE.

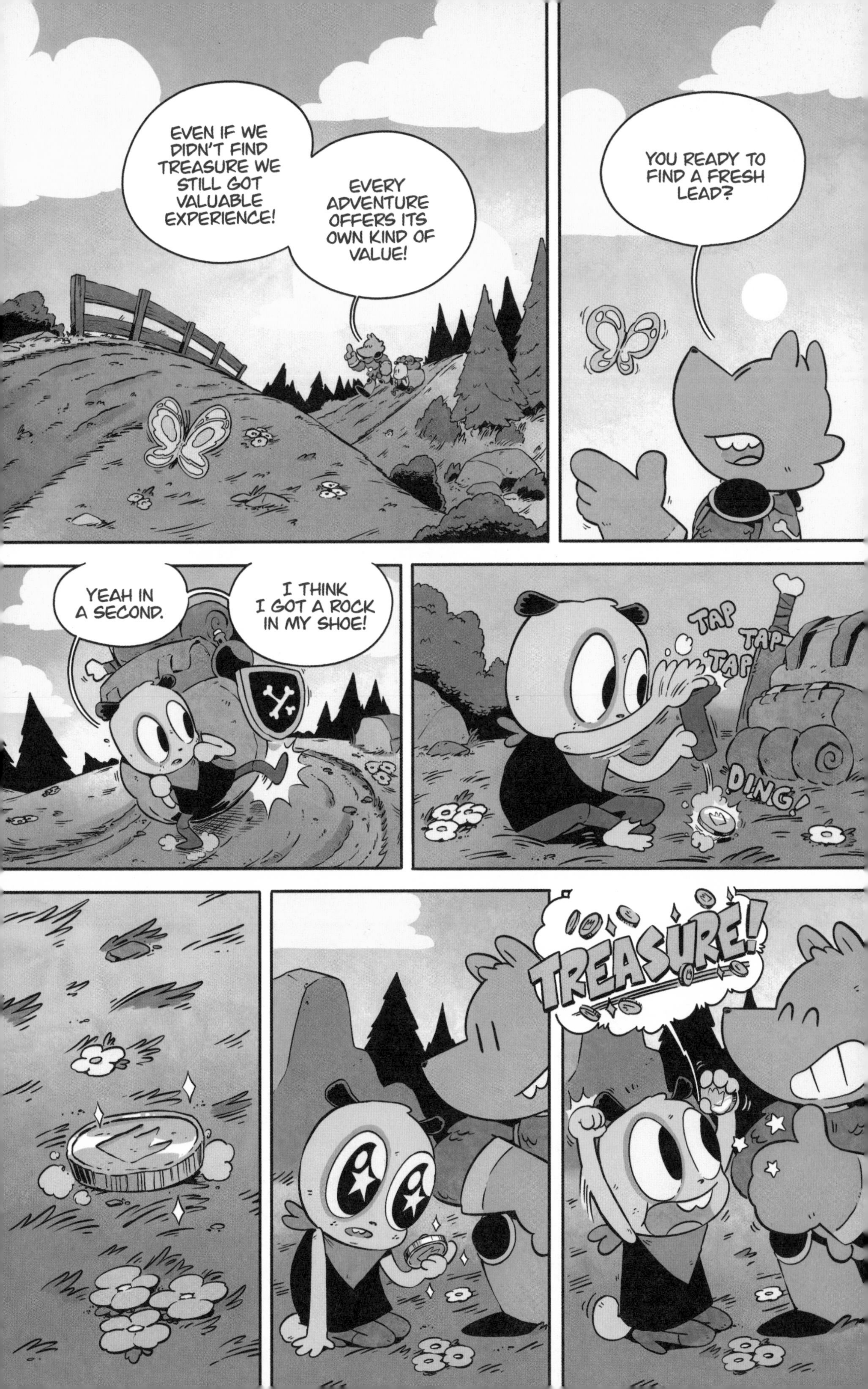
EVEN IF WE DIDN'T FIND TREASURE WE STILL GOT VALUABLE EXPERIENCE!
EVERY ADVENTURE OFFERS ITS OWN KIND OF VALUE!
YOU READY TO FIND A FRESH LEAD?
YEAH IN A SECOND.
I THINK I GOT A ROCK IN MY SHOE!
TAP
TAP
TAP
DING!
TREASURE!

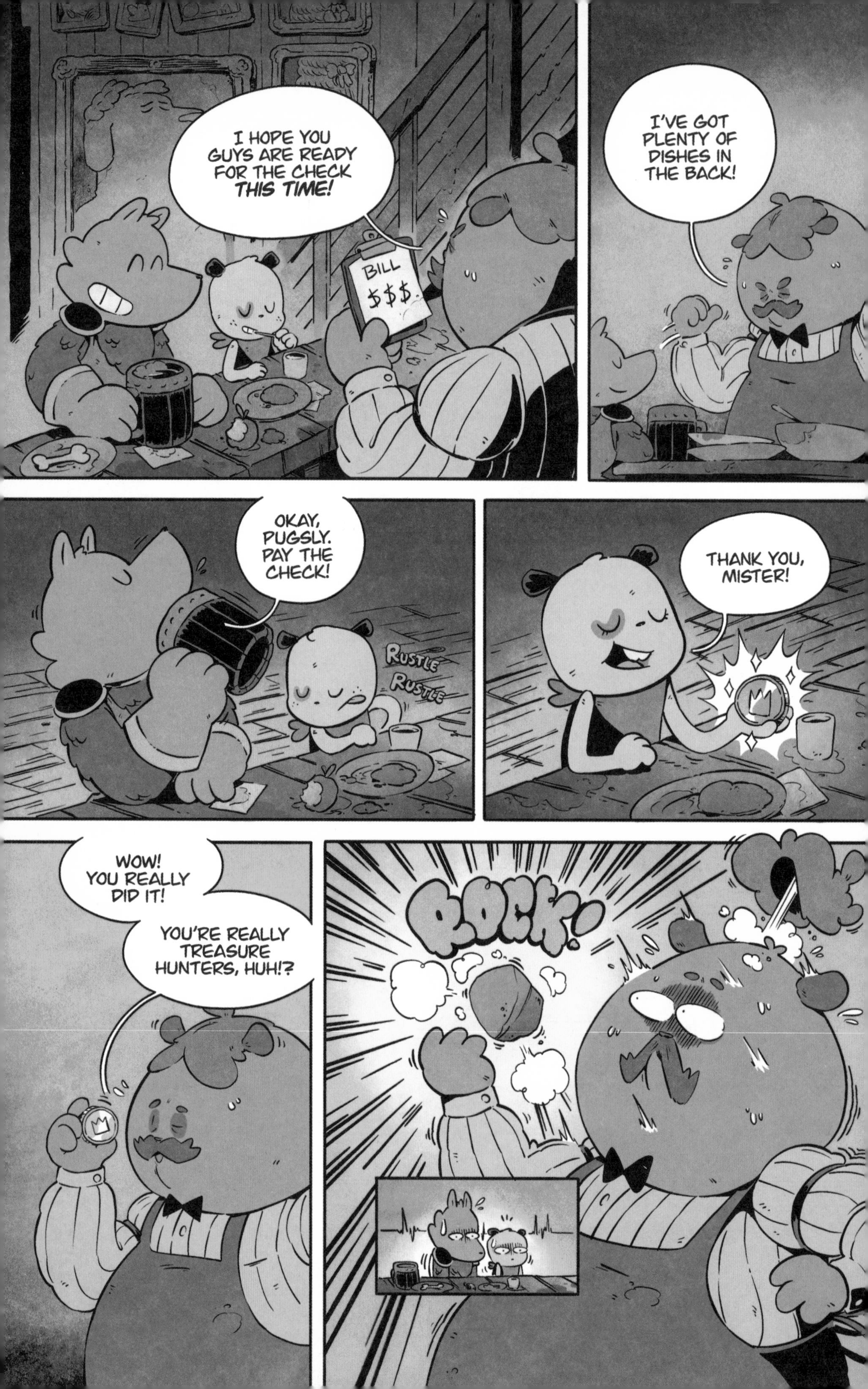
I HOPE YOU GUYS ARE READY FOR THE CHECK THIS TIME!
BILL $$$
I'VE GOT PLENTY OF DISHES IN THE BACK!
OKAY, PUGSLY. PAY THE CHECK!
RUSTLE RUSTLE
THANK YOU, MISTER!
WOW! YOU REALLY DID IT!
YOU'RE REALLY TREASURE HUNTERS, HUH!?
ROCK!

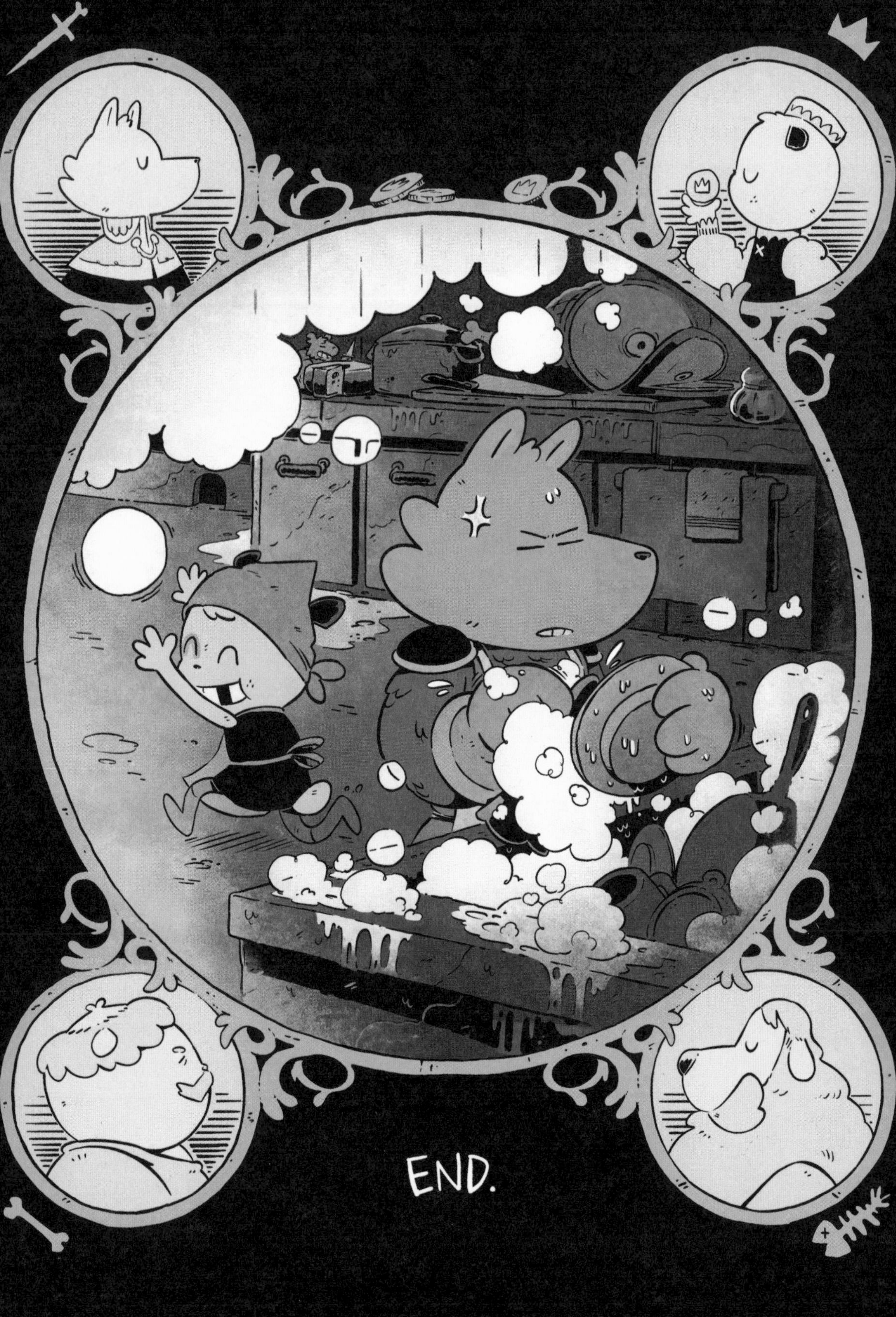

END.

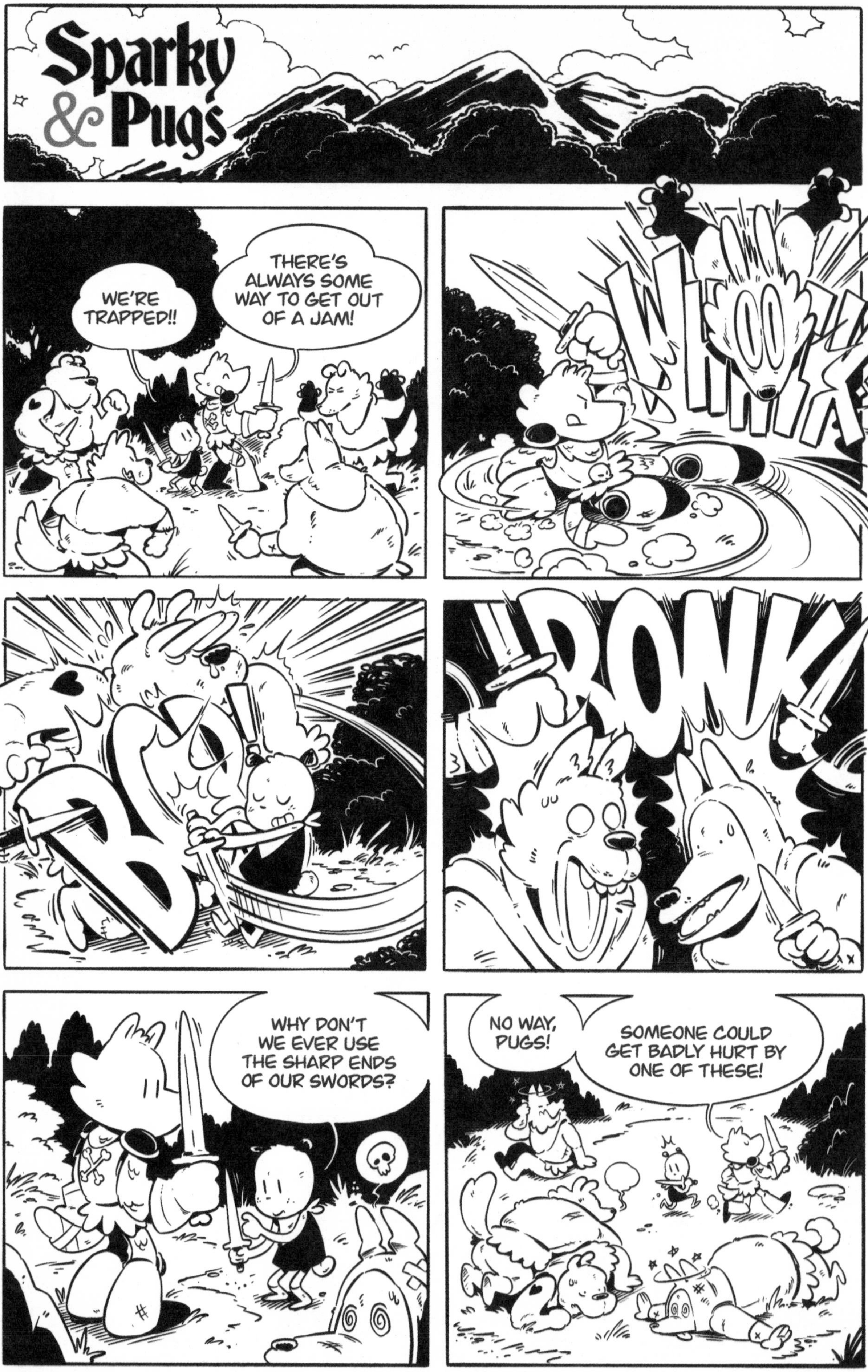
Sparky & Pugs
WE'RE TRAPPED!!
THERE'S ALWAYS SOME WAY TO GET OUT OF A JAM!
WHOOK!!
BOO!
BONK!
WHY DON'T WE EVER USE THE SHARP ENDS OF OUR SWORDS?
NO WAY, PUGS!
SOMEONE COULD GET BADLY HURT BY ONE OF THESE!

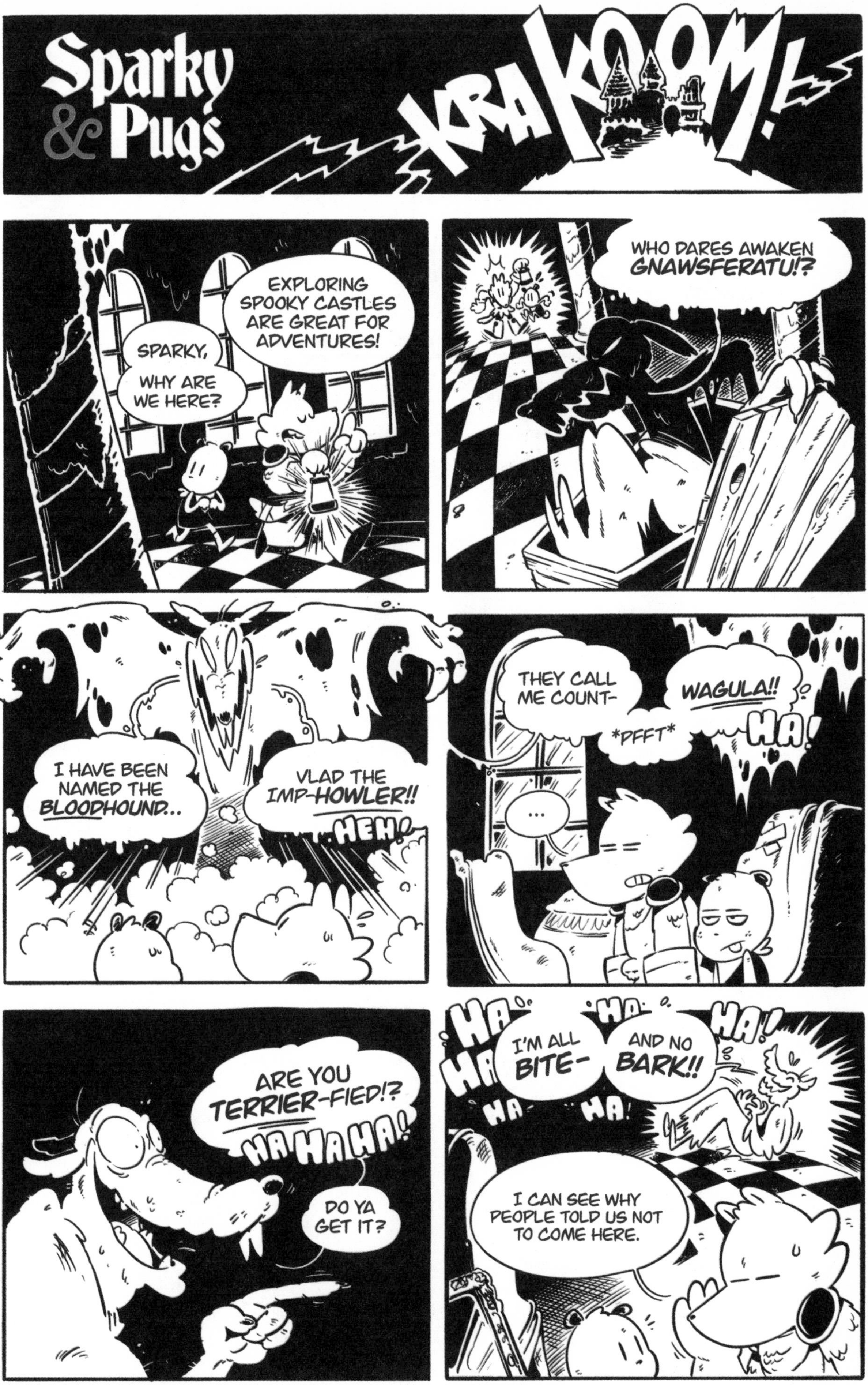

Sparky & Pugs
KRAKOOM!
EXPLORING SPOOKY CASTLES ARE GREAT FOR ADVENTURES!
SPARKY,
WHY ARE WE HERE?
WHO DARES AWAKEN GNAWSFERATU!?
I HAVE BEEN NAMED THE BLOODHOUND...
VLAD THE IMP-HOWLER!!
HEH!
THEY CALL ME COUNT-
WAGULA!!
PFFT
HA!
...
ARE YOU TERRIER-FIED!?
HA HA HA!
DO YA GET IT?
HA HA
I'M ALL BITE-
AND NO BARK!!
HA HA!
HA
HA!
I CAN SEE WHY PEOPLE TOLD US NOT TO COME HERE.

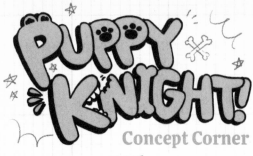

PUPPY KNIGHT!

Concept Corner

THERE ARE MANY THINGS THAT GO INTO MAKING A COMIC, ONE OF WHICH IS MAKING SURE YOU KNOW HOW YOU WANT YOUR CHARACTERS TO LOOK AND BEHAVE!

MICHAEL, WHO CREATED THE CHARACTERS IN ***PUPPY KNIGHT***, WAS IN CHARGE OF ALL INITIAL PASSES IN DESIGNS AND LAYOUTS.

AFTER THE FIRST DRAFT, JOSUE WOULD TAKE THESE IDEAS AND INTERPRET THEM TO THE FINAL ART AND COLORS.

HERE YOU'LL FIND SOME EARLY VERSIONS OF OUR CHARACTER DESIGNS, PAGE LAYOUTS, AND SOME BEHIND-THE-SCENE NOTES!

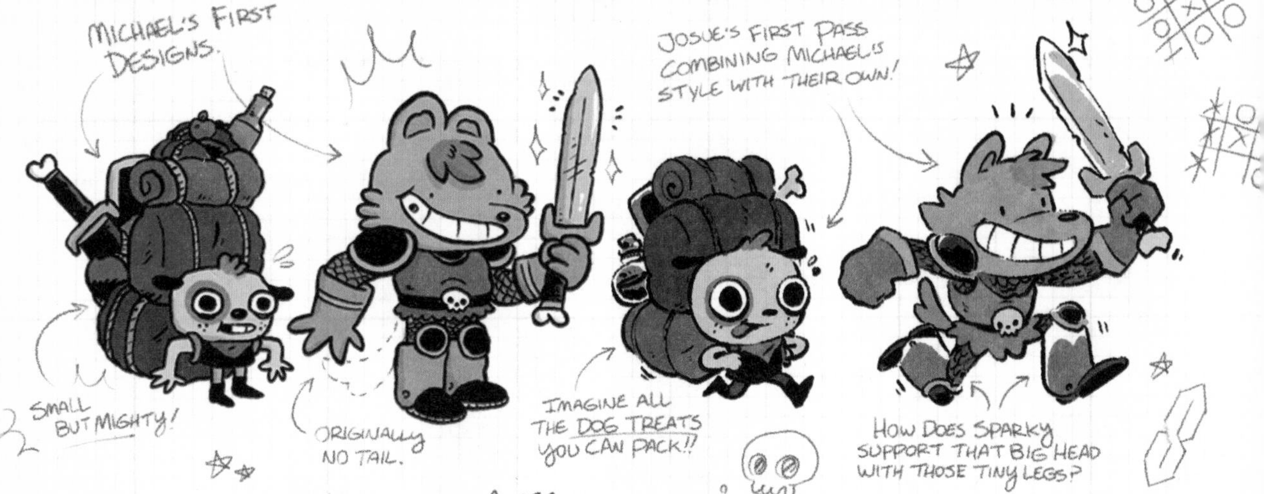

MICHAEL'S FIRST DESIGNS.
JOSUE'S FIRST PASS COMBINING MICHAEL'S STYLE WITH THEIR OWN!
SMALL BUT MIGHTY!
ORIGINALLY NO TAIL.
IMAGINE ALL THE DOG TREATS YOU CAN PACK!!
HOW DOES SPARKY SUPPORT THAT BIG HEAD WITH THOSE TINY LEGS?

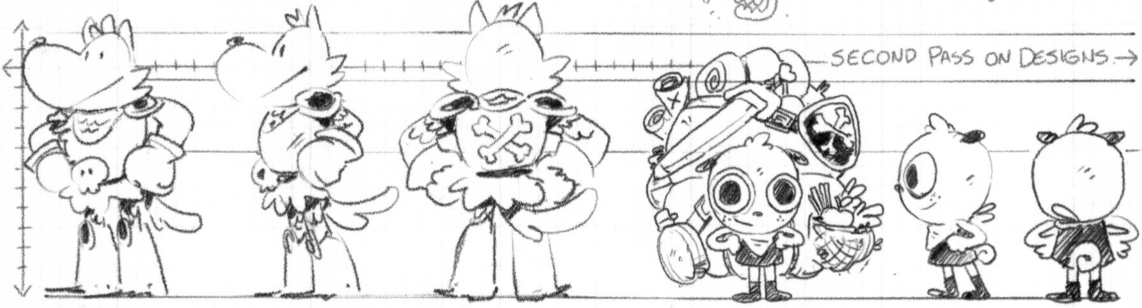

SECOND PASS ON DESIGNS

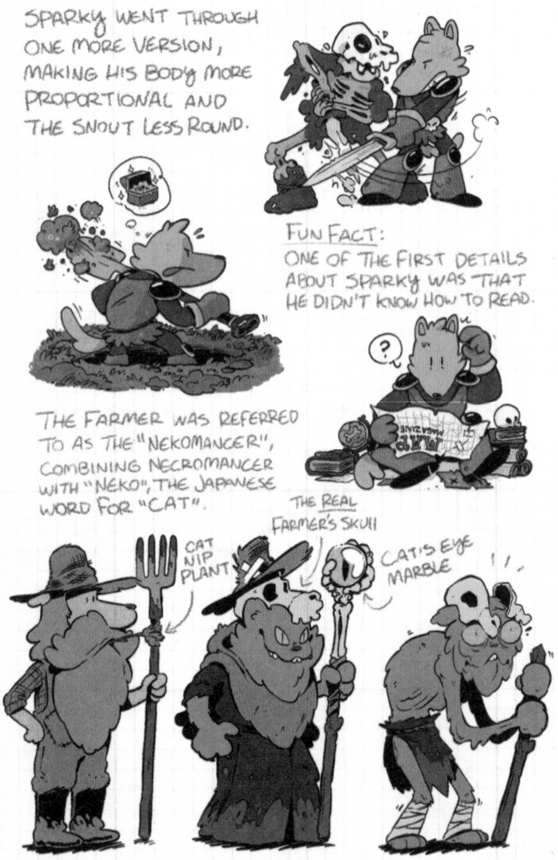

SPARKY WENT THROUGH ONE MORE VERSION, MAKING HIS BODY MORE PROPORTIONAL AND THE SNOUT LESS ROUND.
FUN FACT:
ONE OF THE FIRST DETAILS ABOUT SPARKY WAS THAT HE DIDN'T KNOW HOW TO READ.
THE FARMER WAS REFERRED TO AS THE "NEKOMANCER", COMBINING NECROMANCER WITH "NEKO", THE JAPANESE WORD FOR "CAT".
THE REAL FARMER'S SKULL
CAT NIP PLANT
CAT'S EYE MARBLE

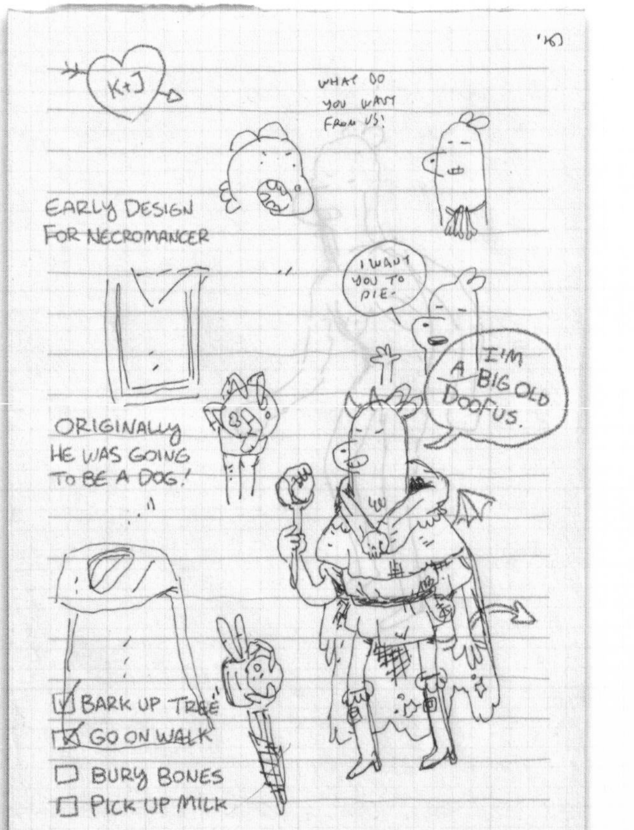

K+J
WHAT DO YOU WANT FROM US!
EARLY DESIGN FOR NECROMANCER
I WANT YOU TO DIE-
I'M A BIG OLD DOOFUS.
ORIGINALLY HE WAS GOING TO BE A DOG!
BARK UP TREE
GO ON WALK
BURY BONES
PICK UP MILK

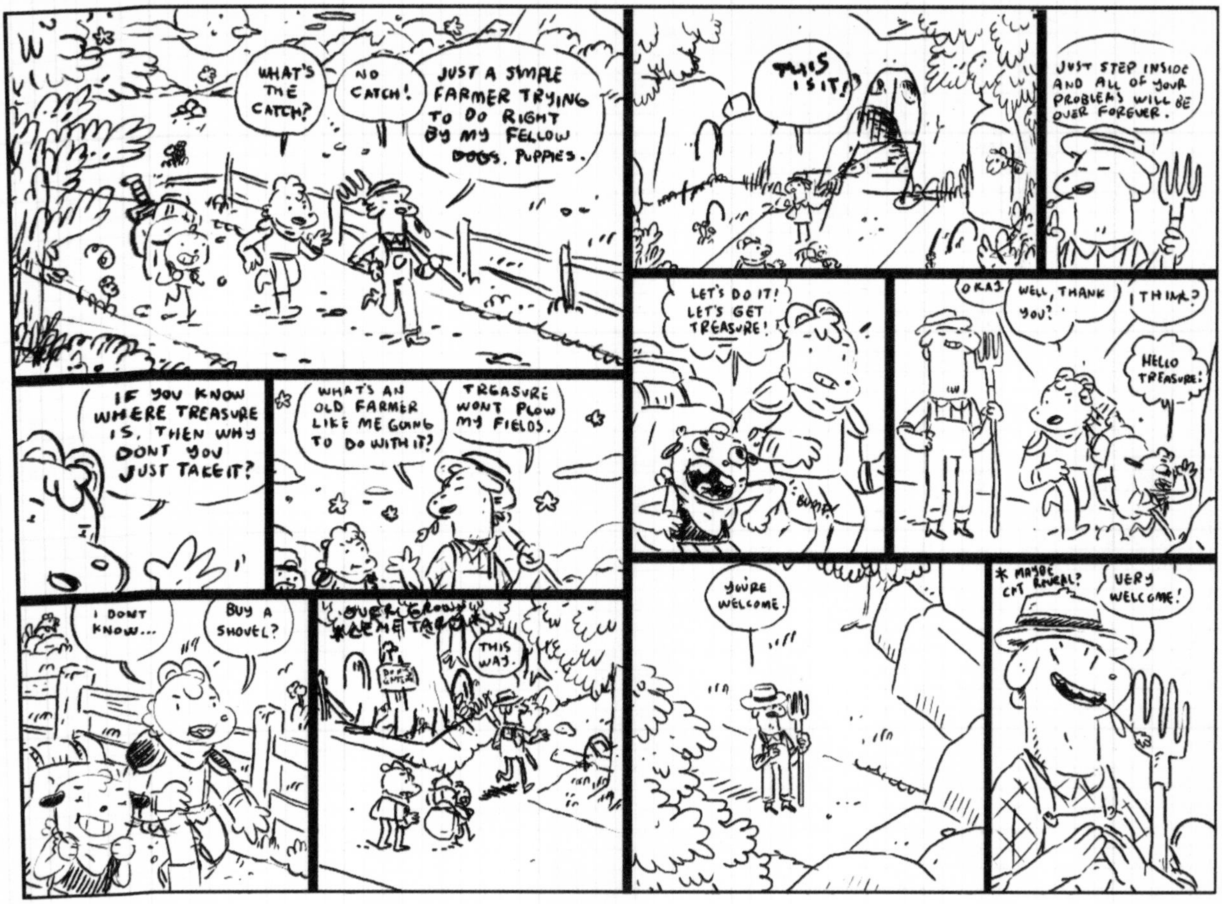
WHAT'S THE CATCH?
NO CATCH!
JUST A SIMPLE FARMER TRYING TO DO RIGHT BY MY FELLOW DOGS. PUPPIES.
IF YOU KNOW WHERE TREASURE IS, THEN WHY DONT YOU JUST TAKE IT?
WHAT'S AN OLD FARMER LIKE ME GOING TO DO WITH IT?
TREASURE WONT PLOW MY FIELDS.
I DONT KNOW...
BUY A SHOVEL?
THIS WAY.
THIS IS IT!
JUST STEP INSIDE AND ALL OF YOUR PROBLEMS WILL BE OVER FOREVER.
LET'S DO IT! LET'S GET TREASURE!
OKAY.
WELL, THANK YOU?
I THINK?
HELLO TREASURE!
YOU'RE WELCOME.
* MAYBE CAT REVEAL?
VERY WELCOME!

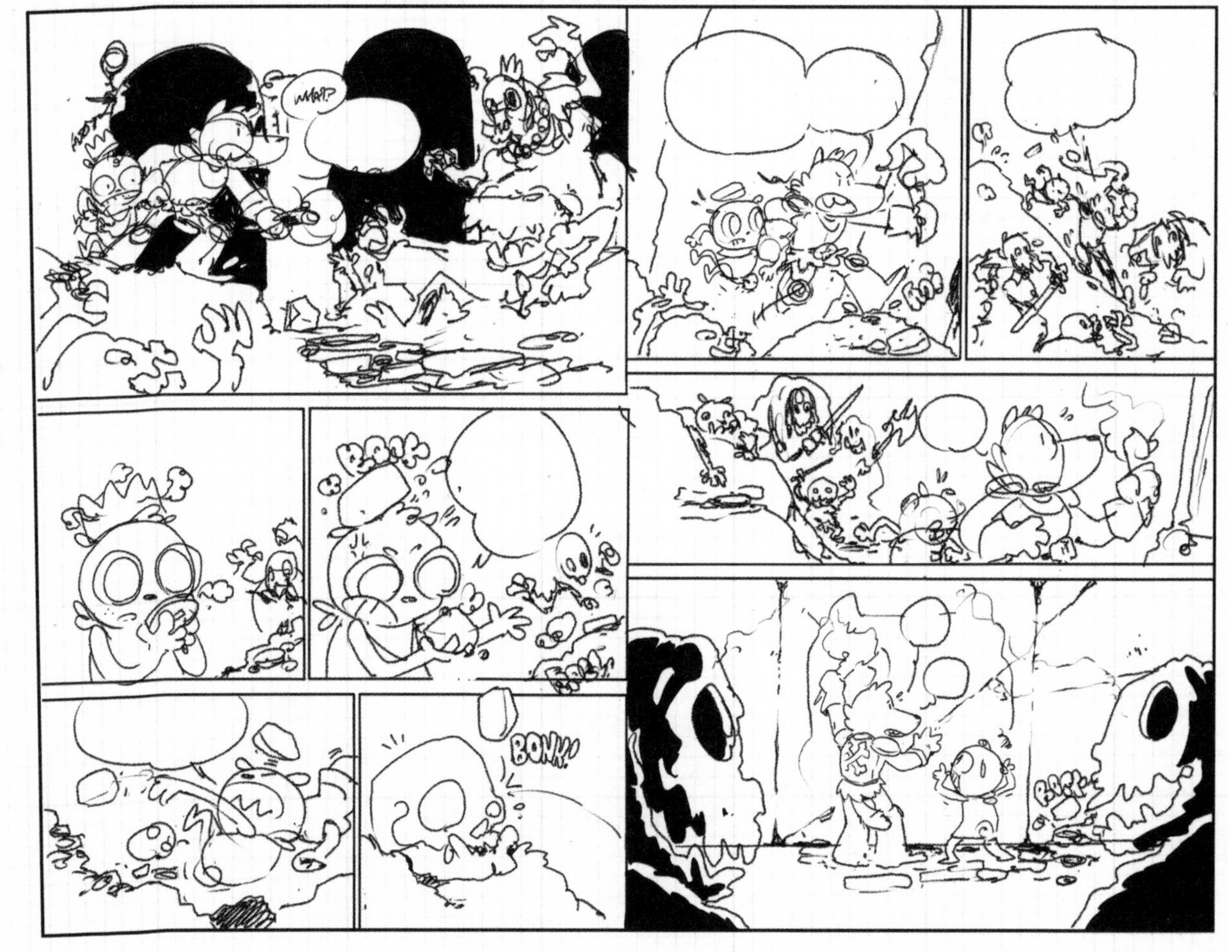
WHAT?
BONK!

Michael Sweater

Michael Sweater is a cartoonist and comics educator living in the Ozark Mountains with his wife, three cats, and one very cowardly dog.

Writing for both children and adults, his main focus is on stories that are highly energetic and deeply sentimental.

He has worked in both comics and animation for Cartoon Network, Oni, Silver Sprocket, Vice, The Nib, and more.

Josue Cruz

Josue (pronounced ho-sweh) Cruz is a budding comic book artist currently based in the Bay Area of California.

Their work is heavily influenced by 90s video games, French comics, and manga—particularly their favorite, One Piece.

Josue hopes to keep creating comics that will make friends, family, and strangers say: "Oh, that's rad."